"IT'S NOT A FACE . . . ONLY A MASK!"
Anne told herself, repeating it; yet the face frightened her. It was a dark mahogany color, parts of which did indeed seem to be made of wood. There was hair, coarse matted grizzled hair, growing out of the face. The hair made a halo around the grimacing face, like a lion's mane. Sprouting from the forehead were two twisted black horns. The face seemed to be smiling, eternally smiling, a horrible evil smile.

"Who is your Master?" bellowed the masked figure.

"You, you are the Master," cried the kneeling hooded figures.

"And who am I?"

"The Devil, the Devil himself!"

ANNE HAD FOUND THE NIGHT-WITCH DEVIL, BUT SHE DID NOT GUESS WHAT THE DEVIL'S WORK WAS TO BE—A SATANIC EXPLOIT THAT WOULD ENDANGER THE WORLD, A PLAN ONLY THE AVENGER COULD FOIL.

Books in This Series

By Kenneth Robeson

Published By

WARNER PAPERBACK LIBRARY

THE NIGHTWITCH
DEVIL

by Kenneth Robeson

**WARNER
PAPERBACK
LIBRARY**

A Warner Communications Company

WARNER PAPERBACK LIBRARY EDITION
First Printing: October, 1974

This Warner Paperback Library Edition is published by arrangement
with The Condé Nast Publications, Inc.

Cover illustration by George Gross

Warner Paperback Library is a division of Warner Books, Inc.,
75 Rockefeller Plaza, New York, N.Y. 10019.

 A Warner Communications Company

Printed in the United States of America

THE NIGHTWITCH DEVIL

CHAPTER I

A Quiet New England Town

MacMurdie didn't know his friend had seen the Devil.

Not at first, not on that chill, rainy morning when he stepped off the train in the quiet New England town of Nightwitch, Massachusetts.

The station, a small and forlorn brown shingle building, was inland from the little Nightwitch harbor which had brought the town its brief spell of prosperity in the last century. There were a few gulls here, though, as brown and forlorn-looking as the ancient station. They sat on its slant roof, huddled.

Mac walked into the little station, which was dim and musty. He carried two medium-sized suitcases. Setting these down, he surveyed the place.

There were two leaks in the roof. A tarnished tin pie pan caught the dripping from one; the other was making a rust-colored pool on the worn wood floor.

7

Hearing a dry cough, Mac turned. "Morning to ye," he said toward the barred counter window.

An ancient white-haired man was hunched there, a station master's cap sitting too far down on his thin head. "Come in on the 10:27, did you?"

"Aye, and now I'd like ta hire a ride."

"Won't" said the very old station master.

"Why is that?"

"Only taxi we had is up on blocks in Nat Hawthorne's garage for the duration," explained the old man. "Any place you want to go, mister, you're more than likely going to have to walk."

As Mac understood it, the friend he'd come to visit lived several miles out of town. Since Mac hadn't been sure what train he'd be able to catch, he had told his friend not to meet him. "Maybe I better make a phone call," he said.

"You can step around here and use the one on the wall," invited the station master. "If you got a nickel to give me."

Mac stepped through the narrow doorway into the old man's office. After locating a coin in his jacket pocket and placing it on the man's rolltop desk, he picked up the phone.

"Who you want to talk to, Eb?"

" 'Tis not Eb speaking," Mac told the operator. "And I'd like you to put me through to Dr. John Ruyle."

After a few seconds the operator said, "What was that name?"

"Ruyle, John Ruyle. He lives out on Stonewall Road."

"I'm afraid we don't have him listed, sir." The phone went dead. Mac frowned around at the old man. "Do ye know Dr. Ruyle?"

The station master's small pale blue eyes looked

8

away. "Name's vaguely familiar, but, nope, I can't say as how I do."

"I know he's got a phone. He told me so in his last letter."

"You figuring to make any more calls, mister?"

Continuing to frown, Mac said, "No, that'll be all, thank ye." He returned to the waiting room and picked up his suitcases. "Is there a hotel in town?"

"There's the Colonial Inn, two blocks north on State Street." The old man, eyes still not meeting Mac's, cleared his throat. "Might be a good idea to take a room there, mister, but . . ."

"But what?"

"Don't mention as how you're here to see that friend of yours."

Mac went striding over to him. "What is it ye know, mon?"

"Nothing, nothing." He backed away from the bars that protected him from Mac.

Shaking his head, the Scot went out into the rain. "'Tis most odd," he said to himself. "I'll leave my luggage at the inn, since it looks like I'll be hiking out to John's place."

The road grew more and more narrow as it turned up into the hills. Trees, newly green, bent low over the roadway, shaking down rain on the trudging MacMurdie.

Mac had known Dr. John Ruyle for a good many years, though he hadn't seen the biologist since he'd come to Massachusetts seven years ago to teach at a large college near Boston. Four months earlier, Ruyle had moved to a large old house here in Nightwitch. He was taking his sabbatical leave and planned to work on a book. The house had been in Ruyle's family for generations and, until his return to it, had stood empty for nearly a decade. Mac, taking a very brief rest from his strenuous career as a member of the Justice, Inc., crime-fighting team, had come to spend a few days as a house-guest of his old friend.

They'd kidded him, especially grinning Cole Wilson about not being able to stand the rural quiet of Nightwitch. MacMurdie, now, had an uncomfortable feeling that he was not destined to have a quiet time of it here. The way the old station master had acted, the way the telephone woman had behaved . . . it gave Mac the feeling, not an unfamiliar one to a man who lived the kind of life he did, that something was going on wrong.

"Woosh!" he exclaimed as he crested the hill and got his first look at the old mansion, " 'tis bigger by far than I expected."

The stone wall that gave the road its name circled the fifteen acres of trees and brush which surrounded the old house. The wall was high, higher than a man, made of large chunks of gray and buff stone. The house sat several thousand feet beyond the high wall—a vast house of stone, turreted, looking as though it had been transported, whole, from some English country estate.

"John always did like his privacy," observed Mac as he headed for the gate.

The black wrought-iron gate stood half open. Thrusting his hands in his pockets, Mac crossed onto the grounds. The rain was falling heavier, spattering down on him. He felt very small with this great forest closing in on him and the vast house looming up ahead of him.

In the center of the heavy oaken front door was set a brass knocker in the shape of an eagle. Mac used it to pound on the wood.

Nothing followed his knocking.

The lean Scot tried again, louder and longer.

Once more there was no response from within the silent house.

Ruyle, in one of his letters, had told him he had a housekeeper. Even if the doctor was out, the woman should be here.

Mac used the knocker a third time, even though he was certain there was no one within.

Then he tried the handle. The big door swung, silently, inward.

Stepping into the long, shadowy hallway, MacMurdie called out, "John, be ye home? 'Tis MacMurdie come to pay a visit."

His words rolled along the hall, bouncing and echoing. Then the silence closed in.

The look of concern deepened on the Scot's face. " 'Tis not right, this."

He began a slow and careful search of the enormous house. It took him nearly an hour. He found nothing—no sign of his friend, or of the housekeeper, and nothing to indicate where either of them might be.

When he returned to his friend's study, the room where he'd commenced his search, Mac noticed something. Only a small thing, a splat of ink on the Oriental carpet beside the desk.

Kneeling, he poked at the black spot. It was still faintly damp. Under the desk, at the back of the kneehole, was a fountain pen. "Perhaps John was writing something and got interrupted," thought Mac.

He searched around on the floor, in the wastebasket. No note or letter did he find.

There was a small envelope-size green blotter, a fresh one, at the edge of the desk top. Mac picked it up and turned it over. There were two lines of writing, in reverse, showing on it. In Ruyle's handwriting, in black ink.

Mac carried the blotter to the window to make out what his missing friend had written.

"There is a Devil," he read, "and I have—"

CHAPTER II

The Devil Himself

The night before, it had also rained. Thunder had rumbled down through the hills around Nightwitch. Lightning crackled, and wind snapped branches off trees.

But that didn't stop the Thirteen from meeting.

Anne Barley was fairly certain they would. She had figured out, in the year she'd been in Nightwitch and working on the *Nightwitch Guardian*, a fairly accurate schedule of when they met.

It hadn't been a year, actually, since the first month or so she hadn't suspected anything. And, as she was an outsider, no one had told her anything openly or even hinted at it. But Anne was very good at sensing things, sensing that something unusual was going on. A conversation she'd walked in on unexpectedly, an accident no one was willing to discuss, an unexplainable run of bad luck for one of the townsmen. After a while, the girl was able to fit some pieces of the puzzle together.

Standing now beneath the beech trees across from the house she was watching, huddled in her dark raincoat, Anne knew she was right.

A few minutes before midnight, the rear door of the saltbox house eased open. A black-cloaked figure came floating out into the stormy night.

Anne moved, following the black shape.

She was also fairly certain where it would lead her. She'd narrowed the possibilities down to two or three. They were moving, through the thick woods and darkness, toward one of those three.

Lightning sizzled, illuminating the night forest.

The black figure was a hundred yards ahead of Anne, cloak fluttering.

"It's going to be at Deacon's Meadow," the girl said to herself. "They'll use the caves at the meadow edge, I'm sure."

She was right about that, too.

The black shape floated straight across the slanting meadow, rustling the high yellow grass. Blackish rocks stood beyond the meadow, then a slaty cliffside. The cloaked figure vanished into a black spot in the cliffside.

Anne stayed crouched behind a twisted oak at the far side of Deacon's Meadow, watching the cave mouth that had swallowed the figure she'd been following. Bringing her wrist close to her face, she saw that it was now midnight. They should all be in there.

Anne was about to leave the shelter of the tree when she heard a rustling. She pressed herself against the rough trunk.

14

Another cloaked figure—this one seemed to be almost flying through the night—was heading for the cave.

"Is that the last of them?" she wondered.

Five minutes went by, then ten. No one else approached the meadow.

Taking a deep breath, holding it, the girl began to make her way, ducked down low, across the meadow. The night wind threw rain at her, clutched at her clothes, tried to spin her around.

She reached the mouth of the cave finally. There was light inside, light and sound. They were chanting, some kind of strange litany.

Anne could not see any of them, for the tunneling entrance of the cave twisted and corkscrewed. Taking another long, and careful, breath, the girl crossed the rocky threshold. "I've come this far," she told herself, "I might as well get a look at the festivities."

". . . he defied the Power," roared a deep rumbling voice inside the cave.

"He defied the Power," repeated other voices.

"He defied the Power and he was struck down," roared the voice.

"He defied the Power and he was struck down."

"Thus will perish all who stand against us."

"Thus will perish all who stand against us."

There was a smell filling the dark tunnel, a sweet, dead smell. Some kind of incense was being burned; a blue smoke came twisting down the rocky passageway.

Anne clapped her hand over her mouth to keep herself from coughing. She halted, pressing her slim back against the stone wall. She could see them now. It made her stop breathing for long seconds.

15

A black altar, streaked with darker stains, stood in the center of the oval cave floor. At each end of the altar silver bowls were smoking and sputtering, spilling the blue smoke into the air.

Kneeling around the altar were a dozen—no, thirteen—thirteen figures. They still wore their cloaks, but even so Anne recognized two others beside the one she had followed.

There was someone on the other side of the black altar. As she watched, the figure stretched up, raising his hands high over his head. The hands were twisted, hairy, and claws seemed to grow from the finger ends. But the face . . . Anne wanted to close her eyes, but she couldn't.

"It's not a face," she told herself, repeating it. "Not a face, only a mask."

She knew that, yet the face frightened her.

It was a dark mahogany color, and parts of it did indeed seem to be made of wood. There was hair, coarse matted grizzled hair, growing out of the face. The hair made a halo around the grimacing face, like a lion's mane. Sprouting from the forehead were two twisted black horns. The face seemed to be smiling, eternally smiling, a horrible evil smile.

"Who is your Master?" bellowed the masked figure.

"You, you are the Master," cried the kneeling figures.

"And who am I?"

"The Devil, the Devil himself!"

Shaking, Anne backed away. Silently she made her way out of there.

Outside she went running across the meadow, never looking back.

"Nothing," said Gil Lunden.

"What do you mean, Gil?" asked Anne, frowning across his office at him.

Lunden was a tall, fair man of thirty-one, a native of Nightwitch, and one of its two attorneys. "I mean, darling, that you should keep quiet about what you saw. Say nothing, do nothing."

She turned away from him and went to the window to watch the wet morning. "I didn't imagine it. I'm not crazy," she said finally.

"Nobody's suggesting that."

"Then something has to be done."

Gil shook his head. "There are a lot of old beliefs still current in towns like Nightwitch."

"This isn't some quaint old folk remedy I'm talking about, Gil," the girl said. "This is witchcraft."

"I'm aware of that, but I don't see any reason to get so upset."

"Upset? When I saw thirteen of my friends and neighbors bowing down to some monstrosity who calls himself the Devil? Upset isn't quite the word for it."

"I've lived here all my life, Anne." Gil left his desk and walked across to her. "Every once in a while you hear a story that somebody's a witch, or that someone has had a hex put on them. It's all pretty harmless, seems to me." He reached out to touch her shoulder.

She shrugged free. "That face, that wasn't harmless," she said. "And, Gil, they were bragging about having struck someone down, struck him down because he defied the Power."

"Look, maybe somebody stubbed his toe and these people are taking credit for it. Nothing very satanic about that, seems to me."

Turning, she looked up into his face. "It just occurs to me," she said, "you already knew about this

17

cult, didn't you? Here I've been poking around, keeping it all secret and playing Nancy Drew. But you . . . you knew about it."

"I hear things," he admitted. "I knew there was some talk about the old beliefs rising up again. You have to realize, Anne, that in wartime, well, some people get very disturbed. If wrapping up in cloaks and pretending to be witches and warlocks helps them forget their troubles, seems to me there's nothing wrong."

"There was nothing playful about what I saw," Anne insisted. "That man, the one who claimed to be the Devil, he was . . . evil."

"You're exaggerating," the young attorney told her. "In our world today people like Hitler are evil, Hitler and his gang. But some harmless guy in a Halloween mask, that's not evil."

"I'm sorry," the girl said, "but I don't agree with you."

"Don't you understand me?" said Gil. "I love you, Anne. I don't want you getting involved with these things."

"I'm already involved. And, Gil, I am going to stay that way." Ignoring his outstretched hand, she went to the door. "If you don't want to help me, I'll find someone who will."

"Now, Anne, why—"

The door slammed on the rest of his words.

Angry, Anne walked down the brick office steps to the street. "Oh, I'm sorry. I was thinking of something else and didn't see you."

The sandy-haired man picked up the suitcase the hurrying girl had knocked from his grip. " 'Tis nothing, lass," he assured her.

They went, for the moment, their separate ways.

18

CHAPTER III

MacMurdie's Quest

You felt snug and comfortable in the editorial offices of the *Nightwitch Guardian*. It was warm, but not too warm; the air was fresh. The editor, a tall rawboned man named Sam Hollis, sat hunched at his desk. He was writing rapidly with a pencil on a yellow legal tablet. Now and then he stopped to chew on the eraser. He finished what he was working on, tore out the page, and then smiled across the desk at Mac. "There, that's taken care of," he said in his slow drawling voice. "Now I can give you my undivided attention, Mr. MacMurdie. How can I help you?"

"It may be ye canna help me at all, Mr. Hollis," said the Scot. He'd been back an hour from the house on Stonewall Road. "I'm nae yet sure I want to go to the police, so I figured as how the editor of the local paper might be the man to see."

Hollis chuckled. "You make me feel like I'm one of these private eyes on the radio," he said. "If I can do anything for you, I'd be glad to. What seems to be the trouble?"

"Do ye know Dr. John Ruyle?"

"Yes," answered the editor. "Can't say I know John well, but I've been out to his place a few times. I like him."

"I came here to Nightwitch to spend a week as John's houseguest," explained Mac. "I'd written telling him the day I was arriving. He's nae at his house, 'tis empty. I'm wondering if something's happened."

Hollis frowned, shaking his head. "No, nothing that I know of. I talked to John on the phone day before—" .

"He does have a phone then?"

"Certainly, what gave you the—"

" 'Twas a lass at the phone exchange, told me he had no phone."

"Must have been Hulda Dolittle. She doesn't take kindly to outsiders." He pushed back from his old desk. "As far as I know, John's had no accident and he wasn't called away suddenly."

"Where mot he be, then?"

The editor walked toward the potbelly stove in the center of the room, holding his palms toward it. "I really don't know what to tell you. You say you were at his house?"

"Aye. He's nae there, nor is—"

The door opened, Anne Barley walked in. "I took a little longer for lunch than usual, Sam. I had something I wanted to check at the library."

"Anne, this is Mr. MacMurdie. Anne Barley, Fergus MacMurdie."

20

Mac rose from his chair. "I believe we bumped into each other earlier."

"Oh, yes. You're the man with the suitcases." The girl dropped her purse on the top of a desk at the side of the room and shrugged out of her raincoat.

"Could it be," suggested Hollis, "that John's ill, her. "Do you have any idea where John might be?"

"Out at that ramshackle mansion of his working on his book." Anne sat down in her desk chair. "John's almost always there."

"He's nae there, Miss Barley, neither John nor his housekeeper."

"Mrs. Dickerson isn't there, either?" asked Anne.

"Does she have people in town? I'd like—"

"Yes, she has some cousins over on the south end of town," said Anne. "What do you think's happened?"

"I dinna know. I'm hoping someone here in Nightwitch can tell me."

"Could it be," suggested Hollis, "that John's ill, and just not answering his door? We've had a lot of flu this past winter."

"I took the liberty of searching his house. There's not anyone there."

Anne asked, "Anything to indicate where he went?"

Mac shook his head, hesitating. "There was one thing," he said. "He seems to have been writing a note when he was interrupted. In the note he refers to someone called . . . the Devil."

Anne made a small gasping sound.

"The Devil?" echoed Hollis.

"Does that mean anything to ye?" Mac looked especially at the girl.

"No, nothing," she said.

21

Hollis rubbed his bony hands together in front of the stove. "John's been working awfully hard on that book of his. You don't think the strain may have . . . ?"

"Nay," said MacMurdie. "John's not the kind of man to have a breakdown." He glanced from one to the other, waited a few seconds. "Well, I'll be going. I want to talk to his housekeeper's people, to see what they can tell me."

Anne left her chair. "It's a difficult house to find, when you're a stranger. Mind if I show Mr. Mac-Murdie the way, Sam?"

The editor smiled. "It's the least we can do."

As they went out into the hall Anne said, very softly, to Mac, "I must talk to you."

The rain churned the gray waters of the small crescent-shaped Nightwitch harbor.

Her eyes on the bay, Anne said, "I haven't told Sam about any of this, Mr. MacMurdie. I suppose I've been enjoying myself playing detective, being a lone wolf."

Mac drank some of his coffee, watching the girl across the restaurant table. "And now ye wish to tell me?"

"I recognized your name," the girl replied, facing him. "You are with Justice, Inc, aren't you?"

"Aye, that I am."

"I didn't say anything about that back at the newspaper office, because I didn't know if you wanted Sam to know who you are."

"You must understand, Miss Barley, that I dinna come here to investigate anything," the Scot explained. "I, honest and true, intended to have a few days of vacation, that's all. Now . . . I'm worried about John."

Anne said, "I'm not sure what's happened to him.

But it's possible he's the one I heard them talking about."

"Them?"

Folding her hands atop the checkered tablecloth, the girl said, "Nightwitch is an old, old town, Mr. MacMurdie. Centuries ago, when the witch craze swept through New England, a cult of witches and warlocks grew up here. Whether you believe in witchcraft and black magic or not, something was pretty certainly going on here. Strange things, things no one could explain." She paused, watching again the gray water. "When they held the witch trials, five citizens of the town were hanged. I've always believed that the judges were as deluded as their poor victims, and yet . . . I'm not so certain any more."

"Do ye mean ye think there is witchcraft being practiced here again?"

"Yes, I do," said Anne slowly. "There is a coven of witches and warlocks, made up of thirteen citizens of the Nightwitch community. They're led by a man calling himself the Devil."

Mac scowled. "Do ye know if John Ruyle was also investigating the activities of this cult?"

"I don't know," she said, "but when you mentioned the note you'd read at the mansion, well . . . that has to be what it means."

"The Devil," said Mac. "Do ye know who he is?"

She said, "I have no idea. I do know who three of the thirteen are. I followed one of the people I suspected of being a member, and that person led me to their coven meeting last night." Anne proceeded to give Mac a detailed account of what she had seen and heard in the cave beyond Deacon's Meadow.

"Aye, all the trappings of the traditional witch cult," said Mac when she was finished.

"What they were saying, about someone having

23

defied the Power and being taken care of . . . I don't know, I'm afraid they might mean John Ruyle."

MacMurdie gave a slow, determined nod of his head. "I'll find out," he said.

CHAPTER IV

Horns and All

Josh Newton, with several large rolled-up maps under his arm, came walking into the Justice, Inc., offices. The black man had a thoughtful look on his face. "Probably only a coincidence," he said.

"Huh?" said the gigantic Smitty, who was sitting in a chair near the windows. He was tinkering with the portable radio that rested on his vast lap. "What's a coincidence?"

The black man spread two of the maps out on the rug, weighting down the edges with an ashtray and some books. "I've been doing a study, at Dick's suggestion, of the incidents of sabotage in various parts of the country. Here's the map for part of New England."

Cole Wilson was the only other member of Justice, Inc., in the Bleek Street headquarters at the moment. Grinning, he strolled over to look down at

25

Josh's map. "Looks like an outbreak of measles right there."

"I marked each act of sabotage—to a defense plant, shipyard, military base, and so on—with a red dot," explained Josh. "You'll notice that the area enclosed in that circle has had a pretty high rate of trouble in the past twelve months."

"Whereabouts is that?" asked Smitty.

"Massachusetts," replied Josh. "Funny thing is, the town of Nightwitch is right on the edge of the circle."

"Hey, that's where Mac is staying," realized Smitty.

His grin widening, Cole said, "So Mac's landed smack dab in the middle of a nest of spies and saboteurs? As I've often pointed out, it's impossible for any of us to really take a vacation."

"Not implying there are any saboteurs based in Nightwitch," said Josh. "What I said was, it's a co-incidence, most likely. Nightwitch just happens to be on the edge of an area where there's been a lot of sabotage activity lately."

"Mac'll spot anything funny-looking," said the giant, returning to his tinkering.

"He already has." Richard Henry Benson had entered the room. He was a young man, in years, but there was nothing really youthful about him. He had a grim, determined look, and he radiated a kind of confidence seldom seen in younger men. There was no doubt, once you'd seen him, as to who headed up the crack crime-fighting organization known as Justice, Inc.

"You don't mean to say," asked Cole, "that Fergus has already uncovered a nest of spies?"

The Avenger seated himself behind his desk. "It's something a bit stranger than that," he told the trio.

26

"Mac believes there's a witch cult functioning in Nightwitch."

"Ah, he's got a more colorful imagination than I suspected," remarked Cole.

"Hold on, Cole," warned Smitty. "Mac doesn't have hallucinations. If he says there's witches, then there's witches."

Josh asked, "How'd Mac find out about them?"

"He suspects they may have had something to do with the fact that the friend he went to visit has disappeared," said Benson.

"That Doc Ruyle guy, you mean?"

"Right, Smitty. John Ruyle has vanished." The Avenger went on to tell them what MacMurdie had said when he'd phoned him a half-hour before.

"Not only witches," said Cole when Benson had finished his narrative, "but the Devil, horns and all."

"It's no joke," said Smitty. "It sounds like these witches maybe knocked off Mac's buddy."

Josh said, "Nightwitch, as you might guess from its name, figured in the witchcraft trials in the late Seventeenth century. But beliefs like that, in witchcraft and sorcery, were supposed to have died out centuries ago."

"Could it have hung on?" asked Smitty. "In certain out-of-the-way places?"

"I've seen," said Cole, "some fairly backward New England towns."

"But Nightwitch," put in Josh, "did pretty well as a shipping town about a century ago. It expanded for a time, got in a lot of new people. What I'm getting at is that old-time beliefs and practices are more likely to hang on in a town that's stagnated for centuries. Nightwitch hasn't, exactly."

His fingers steepled beneath his chin, the Avenger said, "There are several reasons for reviving a witch cult, not all of them having to do with a belief in magic and Satanism. Cole, I'd like you and Smitty to go up to Nightwitch. Give Mac a hand digging into this business." He paused for a few seconds. "You might take those maps of Josh's along with you."

CHAPTER V

The Witches

It was true what they said about time. You needed outside clues to keep track of it.

Here, in the absolute blackness of the small stone room, he had no idea what the time was. No idea how long he'd been a prisoner.

"Several days," guessed Dr. John Ruyle. "I've been down here several days."

He wasn't certain why he thought his prison was down. A feel, chiefly, that this small stone cell was underground.

He believed also he was near the water. Sometimes he could hear the sea, the tide.

"Should be able to keep track of time by the tides," he told himself.

The trouble was, he slept sometimes. And he never knew for how long.

"And you don't know," he reminded himself,

"how long you were unconscious after they dumped you down here."

He'd been writing at his desk, starting to put down what he'd learned so far about the witch cult. He was aware, for seconds only, of a strange, sweet smell. He went to sleep, head falling toward the desk top.

When he awakened, he was here.

"Wherever here is."

The room was roughly square, judging from the measurements he'd been able to pace off in the dark. Ten feet across, with the ceiling about ten feet above.

Ruyle had been able to locate a few cracks in the walls, long, thin cracks which might indicate concealed doors. He'd been unable to force anything open. And there was no trace of a real, full-fledged door or window.

Once a day, or possibly more often, a tiny grating near the floor opened. A cup of water and two dry biscuits were shoved in to him.

No light came in with the food. In fact, the first time the meal had been pushed into the stone room, Ruyle had no idea what it was. He felt around in the dark, after hearing the grating open and shut, and found the earthenware mug of water and the hard biscuits.

"They apparently want me to stay alive," Ruyle concluded now as he roamed the blackness. "But for how long?"

He had suspected the existence of the witch cult for several months. He'd begun, very cautiously he thought, to gather facts about the group. He was fairly certain he knew the identities of four and possibly five of the thirteen members of the coven. He

30

even had a suspicion as to the identity of the man who called himself the Devil.

Somehow, though, they'd found out, they'd learned he was suspicious and was stalking them. It was too soon, because Dr. Ruyle had intended to tell MacMurdie all he'd learned.

"Mac!" said Ruyle suddenly. "He must be here by now. Surely that much time has gone by."

He felt more hopeful. Mac would do something, would find him down here.

"Won't he?" Ruyle asked the darkness.

There was no rain that night, only a fine mist.

MacMurdie eased open his bedroom window, stepped out on the ledge, and dropped to the grassy lane ten feet below.

Most of the town seemed to be asleep.

The bells in the old church steeple sounded, indicating it was eleven-thirty.

Mac made his way down the lane, away from the inn and out to the street. Anne Barley had drawn him a map to show him how to get to Deacon's Meadow, how to get there the least traveled way. The girl thought the coven would be meeting again tonight, and Mac didn't want to run into any of them while they were en route.

The mist swirled around him, dampening his face, chilling him. The scent of the sea was strong all around. Mac stopped all at once and pressed into a dark doorway.

A thickset fisherman went stumbling by, singing to himself. Not a sea chantey, something from the "Hit Parade." He didn't notice MacMurdie.

A moment later the Scot resumed his journey. He encountered no one else in the silent town. Soon he was away from the streets and the low buildings, out in the countryside.

The thickening mist rubbed at every thing, blurring the fields and the twisted trees, muffling the cries of night birds.

Mac felt as though he had the whole of the twisting hillside road to himself; indeed, it was as though he had the whole world to himself. There was nothing but misty silence.

Then he heard something. Very faint, off to his right.

At first he thought it might be an animal, whimpering.

"Nae, 'tis a woman," he decided, listening more carefully. "Aye, a woman in trouble, from the sound of her."

It was a sobbing, a dry, even sobbing, a hopeless sound.

There were trees all along this side of the roadway, maples, oaks. The trees grew close together, branches interlocked. Narrowing his eyes, the Scot tried to see where the crying woman was.

The sobbing continued.

MacMurdie always carried a small flashlight with him. He knew it wouldn't do any good in this mist—all he'd get would be a reflection of the beam. Carefully, he stepped off the road and made his way through the dark trees.

He saw her, huddled on the ground beneath a tree, holding tight to herself. She rocked back and forth as she cried, like a mourner at an old country funeral.

Approaching her, Mac said, "What's wrong?"

The sobbing stopped. The woman stood up, drew her dark cloak tighter around her. She laughed.

CHAPTER VI

A Long Vigil

Anne Barley sat up in the armchair, awake again.

The dawn light showed at the windows of her cottage. She brushed her hair back, then compared the time showing on her wristwatch with that of the mantel clock.

"After six-thirty," she said. She stood up, stretching. She'd dozed, this last time, for almost two hours. "And still no sign of him."

MacMurdie had been made to promise, no matter how late it was, he'd stop by at her cottage when he returned from Deacon's Meadow. Anne had wanted to accompany him, but the Scot had vetoed that.

"I should have insisted," she said, pacing the small parlor. "Those meetings never last more than two hours, usually."

She went to a window and looked out at the beginning day. There was no rain, no mist. The sun would show today. "He may have gotten lost," she reflected.

It hardly seemed likely. A man like MacMurdie, a man who'd been with Justice, Inc., since its founding, wouldn't get lost.

"They've done something to him." She stayed, very still, beside the window and watched the lane.

When the church bells rang, she realized it was seven. She'd been standing there almost a half-hour. "He's not coming," she said, biting at her knuckle.

It was possible, of course, MacMurdie simply hadn't kept his promise. He might have gone straight to the inn when he returned to town last night. He might be there now.

Anne hurried into the hall to her phone. "Oh, yes, good morning, Hulda."

"You're up bright and early, Annie," replied the phone operator.

"So are you." Mrs. Dolittle seemed to be on the job no matter when you picked up the phone. "Can you connect me with the inn, please?"

"No sooner said than done, Annie."

After five rings a weary voice answered, "Good morning, Colonial Inn."

"I'd like Mr. MacMurdie's room, please."

"A mite early in the day to be disturbing him, don't you think?"

"It's very important."

"Well, hang on and I'll buzz him."

The phone in MacMurdie's room rang a half-dozen times, and a half-dozen more.

"That's enough to wake the dead," said the clerk. "I'd say he ain't in."

"All right, thank you."

"Any messages for—"

Anne hung up. "I'll wait a bit longer. Yes, and

34

then I'll . . . what?" She wasn't sure what she should do next.

Nightwitch had a police chief, and an assistant police chief. Anne didn't think they could be of much help, but she might have to go to them if she couldn't think of anything else to do.

She waited fifteen minutes more, then threw on a tan coat and left the cottage.

The coupe pulled up beside her, its old brakes causing it to swing slightly to the left. "Anne, what are you doing out here?"

The girl, who was on foot, halted at the side of the winding country road. "Good morning, Gil."

The young attorney set the brake, switched off the motor, and climbed out of the car. "I've got an early appointment with old man Millman," he said. "Where are you going?"

"It doesn't concern you."

"Of course it does," he said. "Does it have something to do with this so-called gathering of witches?"

"You'll be late. Mr. Millman will be annoyed."

"He's always annoyed, no matter what time I get there. Are you going to Deacon's Meadow?"

"Yes, I am."

"Why?"

"I think the so-called witches may have done something to a friend of mine."

"What do you——"

"Never mind, Gil. You think it's all a fantasy, some kind of hallucination of mine. So go on about your business."

"You're my business," he said. "You're so preoccupied with witches and spooks, Anne, you seem to have forgotten that we're engaged."

35

"Informally."

"Okay, informally, until I find out for sure whether I'm going to be drafted or not," said Gil. "But engaged."

She looked up at him. "Will you, please, help me?"

After a second of hesitation, he answered, "Yes, Anne."

"Come up there to the meadow with me. I want to see if I can find any trace of Mr. MacMurdie."

"Who exactly is MacMurdie?" He opened the passenger door for her.

As they drove up into the hills she told Gil about MacMurdie and what he'd set out to do.

"You mean you think this bunch has done something to Dr. Ruyle, too?"

"Yes."

"I really don't know what to think," said the lawyer. "It seemed to me that playing at witchcraft was harmless, not anything to—"

"Wait now, Gil," said the girl. "You told me you did know about this coven even before I mentioned it to you."

Keeping his eyes on the road, Gil replied, "I've lived here most of my life, Anne. Lately, sure, I've heard a few rumors, but nothing to indicate—"

"Yet you gave me the impression you thought I was an idiot."

"I didn't feel it'd do you any good to tangle with these people. Believe me, I thought they were only playing games with some old-time superstitions."

"A gathering of witches isn't the same thing as a quilting bee," said the girl. "Do you know who the members are?"

"I could probably guess at least a few."

"Do you know who the Devil is?"

"No."

"You can't guess?"

"No."

Anne slowly sighed out her breath. "Honestly, Gil, what did you think they were up to? I mean they've been holding Black Masses, Lord knows what else."

"Old people, simple people, they need something to divert them," he said. "I really think this is—"

"Honestly, Gil. You can't be that naive. These people, and they certainly aren't all little old ladies, are vicious."

"All right, I'm a simple rustic." He pulled the car over to the edge of a field. "We'll have to walk from here."

Anne jumped from the coupe before he got around to help her. "But you're not stupid, Gil. That's why I can't understand how—"

"Maybe I have other things on my mind." He followed her up through the slanting field. "Such as trying to plan for the future—our future, I mean."

They found only silence when they reached the cave at Deacon's Meadow.

Gil went in first, clicking on the flashlight he'd brought from his car. "No sign of anything here," he said after a moment.

"They have their altar right . . ." Anne lowered her hand.

There was no altar there now.

"Whatever was here is gone now." Gil shone the light on the spot she'd pointed at.

"But there are scratches there, in the earth."

37

Anne moved closer to the circle of yellow light. "You can see where it stood. And there's something . . ." Kneeling, she moved her hand across a black patch on the cave floor. "What is it?"

Her fingers were stained a darkish red. "Blood," she said.

CHAPTER VII

Missing Persons

"Spring is nigh," observed Cole, putting his knee up against the dashboard.

Frowning out at the pale yellow midday, Smitty said, "Not nigh enough."

"Nightwitch three miles," read Cole from a signpost. "Via that road there."

Smitty swung their car onto the side road. "What do you think we're going to find in this burg?"

"I have a fervent hope that it's a damsel in distress. To me an investigation, no matter how stimulating a problem it presents, is nothing unless there is a charming young girl somewhere close to its center."

"What I'm getting at," said the giant, "is do you think they got witches?"

"Witches, warlocks, and Mr. Lucifer Satan in person, according to Fergus."

39

The big man glanced round at the bleak fields, the trees that hadn't yet begun to bud. "Two or three hundred years ago, I guess, they all believed in that black magic stuff around these parts."

"At least a dozen of them—a baker's dozen, that is— apparently believe in it right now today."

"I don't think there can really be witches," said Smitty. "Any magic that's going to be worked nowadays, it's going to be done by scientists. You take, for example, the possibilities of atomic energy. Why, I bet—"

"Colonial Inn coming up on our right."

Smitty guided the car into a parking place on the small town square. "What about the spy angle on this thing?" he said as he turned off the ignition.

"I'd say there has to be one."

"Yeah, what makes you so sure?"

Easing out of the car, Cole said, "Richard seems to have a hunch there's a connection between Mac-Murdie's hobgoblins and the increasing sabotage rate in this part of New England. I have a great deal of faith in his hunches."

Smitty scratched his head. "Maybe so."

Cole was studying the statue of a Civil War general that stood on a high pedestal at the square's center. Several seagulls were resting on the general's shoulders and hat. "There are a good many things you can use a quiet harbor town for," he said. "And now let's join Mac."

The lobby of the inn was filled with furniture of the last century, bentwood rockers, plump Morris chairs, marble-top tables. The small middle-aged clerk had come out from behind the reception desk to stand with his back to the empty fireplace.

"Yes, gentlemen?" he asked.

"We'd be obliged," grinned Cole, "if you'd announce our arrival to Mr. MacMurdie."

From an easy chair in a dim corner of the room came a cough. A thin, sparse-haired man rose up out of the chair. "Would you be friends of Mr. MacMurdie's?" he asked.

"Friends," replied Cole, "and colleagues."

The thin man rubbed at his head, then poked his finger into the left-hand pocket of his gray vest. "Name is Miller Storm," he told them. "I'm chief of police."

Frowning, Smitty said, "Where's Mac?"

Chief Storm said, "Was hoping you could tell me."

"Isn't he here?"

"Nope."

"Went off late last night," put in the little clerk, getting behind his desk. "Nobody's seen him since. All sorts of folks been asking after him. Some girl I think was that Miss Barley, and Sam Hollis over to the newspaper. I begin to wonder what was up, so to speak."

"Burt went and took a look around Mr. MacMurdie's room," said the chief. "Called me next."

Cole asked, "Something wrong in the room?"

"Nope," said Chief Storm, " 'cept your friend ain't in it."

"We'd like to have a look ourselves," said Cole.

"No reason why not. Won't tell you nothing though."

Smitty crossed the lobby to the desk. "You say Mac went out someplace last night?"

The clerk swallowed. "I didn't see Mr. MacMurdie myself," he said. "But Wally Reisberson—he does some cleaning up for us—told me he saw him jump out of his window at about midnight."

"Most interesting," said Cole.

"Any idea what your friend was up to?" Chief Storm asked.

"I must admit to being completely baffled," answered Cole. "My associate, Mr. Smith, and I are traveling to Boston on business. Knowing that Mr. MacMurdie was vacationing here, we decided to pay him a visit."

Chief Storm asked, "Know Dr. Ruyle?"

"It seems to me Mr. MacMurdie mentioned him. What does he have to say about the situation?"

"Got no idea. Ruyle's missing, too. So's his housekeeper. Found that out 'bout an hour ago."

"Baffling," said Cole.

The chief of police looked from Cole to Smitty. He twisted his finger around in a vest pocket, saying finally, "Show you his room now. Come along."

CHAPTER VIII

Premature Burial

"By the tartan of old Rob Roy MacGregor," said Mac, "they gulled me good and proper."

He shook his head again and blinked his eyes.

There was almost no light in the room he'd found himself in. A sliver of sunlight found its way in by way of a thin crack in the vaulted marble ceiling.

"Woosh," remarked the Scot, "I ne'er thought I'd get a look at the inside of me own tomb."

For that's where he was, in a crypt. The thick walls were of real marble. There were marble shelves on three of the walls, no windows. Five coffins, ornate, of ebony and gold, sat on the shelves.

MacMurdie had come to fifteen minutes before. From the look of the feeble light seeping in, it was morning. There was a sore spot at the base of his skull. Mac remembered doing battle with at least three cloaked figures there in the woods. The woman had laughed, then the three had jumped him. Three to one didn't faze the belligerent Scot, and he'd felled one of the cloaked men when someone hit him from behind with a blackjack.

"I wonder if 'twas the laughing lass who sapped me."

Across the tomb, up three marble steps, was a heavy metal door. It was locked, Mac had discovered that already. He also found that everything he'd had in his pockets was gone. He had nothing on him with which to pick the lock. They'd even taken his belt, the buckle of which contained a compact two-way radio.

"Well, I'm still pretty lively, for an inmate of a tomb," said MacMurdie. "I'll nae give up yet."

He began another slow, careful circuit of the room. There were two copper lamps bolted to the wall. "Might be able to unscrew those and use them as a weapon on whoever comes to look after me."

That was only an assumption, Mac reminded himself. No one might ever come to him again. They might have left him here to die of starvation.

Mac moved to the nearest coffin. He should be able to fashion a piece of one of those hinges into a lockpick. First, though, he'd have to get it loose from the coffin lid.

Crouching, Mac scanned the floor to see if anything had been dropped there.

"Hoot," he exclaimed, "what do ye make of that?"

There were numerous muddy footprints on the marble floor. Some looked quite fresh; others were weeks old. There were prints from different-size shoes and from boots.

"For a tomb, there's quite a bit of traffic."

Mac followed the freshest set of footprints. They

44

led him to the blank wall. All the other prints seemed to dead-end there, as well. Several of the muddy prints were cut in half by the marble wall.

"Unless these lads have picked up the handy knack of walking through walls," observed Mac, "there's a way to swing this wall open."

He decided to find it.

"I'm worried about her," said Sam Hollis. The newspaper editor was standing near his potbellied stove, which was cold today.

"For a small town," observed Cole, "you have a lot of missing persons."

"Oh, Anne's probably not missing," said Hollis with a nervous chuckle. "But . . . well, I don't really know where she is. That is, I only know where she isn't."

"You said," said Smitty, "you were worried."

"I have a feeling Anne's mixed up in something," answered Hollis. "Some odd things have been going on in Nightwitch lately. John Ruyle's disappearance, followed by MacMurdie's. Anne knows more about that than she's told me, I'm pretty sure."

Cole asked him, "Where was she supposed to be?"

"Well, she came in here about three hours ago," said the editor. "Looked sort of upset, like she was trying to make up her mind about something. Of course, maybe she'd just had a quarrel with her young man, I wasn't sure. Anyhow, we got a call there'd been some kind of boating accident down in the harbor near Frenkel's Boatyard. They had the victims in the boatyard proper. I was going to trot down, it's a couple miles from here, but Anne said she'd cover the story and take some pictures."

"And it doesn't usually take her three hours to do a job like that?" Smitty said.

45

"Anne's not like your average lady writer," said Hollis. "She's fast and efficient."

Cole moved toward the office door. "What about the beau you mentioned?"

"That's Gil Lunden, up and coming young lawyer he is," said Hollis. "Matter of fact, I just now called him to see if Anne was maybe with him. Girl who does his typing said he was out seeing the widow Waxman about her will. Not likely he'd take Anne along."

"We better see what they know down at that boatyard," suggested Smitty. "How do we get to the joint?"

"Yes, that's a good idea," said the editor. "I tried to telephone, but nobody's answering." He gave them instructions on how to find the boatyard. Then he asked, "What's all this about? I don't like to pry, but I wouldn't be a newspaperman if I wasn't a curious bird."

"You've been very helpful," said Cole. "We can't, though, tell you anything until we find Mac."

"I smell a story," said Hollis.

"I smell something, too, but I'm not sure what it is." Cole opened the door, and he and the giant left.

CHAPTER IX

A Bit Of A Struggle

"Dismal," remarked Cole.

A clammy mist was rising off the choppy waters of the Nightwatch bay. It seemed to come stumbling in huge billows toward them as they walked toward the boatyard.

"Not a picture postcard view," agreed Smitty.

A bedraggled-looking seagull was staggering along the oily planks of the boardwalk which led to the high wood fence around the yard.

"Not unless you're used to having Gustave Doré do your postcards," said Cole. "I don't notice any evidence of the presence of our sought-after sob sister."

"Naw, this joint looks like it's been closed up since Hector was a pup." Smitty reached out a huge hand and rattled the rusty padlock on the boatyard gate.

Eyes narrowed, Cole took in their surroundings. There was nothing around here but a few old shacks which were leaning against each other for support and a baitshop with a clocksign in its door promising to be back at 2. The broken windows indicated the promise would not be kept. "Does it occur to you, Smitty, that Miss Barley may have been lured here for some purpose other than a newspaper yarn?"

The giant's head bobbed. "Yeah, it's starting to look like that."

"Think you might be able to boost me over the fence?"

"I can pick you up and toss you over."

"A boost will suffice," said Cole. "I want to make sure nobody is in there."

"Don't seem likely." Bending, Smitty cupped his hands together.

Cole stepped aboard and was lifted up until he could grasp the fence top. "Well, up, up, and away," he said as he climbed over.

He landed, wide-legged and flat-footed, on the patch of weedy ground. When he faced around he said, "Don't actually want to buy a boat, merely browsing."

"Nice and easy, raise up your hands, palsy-walsy," instructed the thick-necked man who stood confronting him. He wore a peajacket, bellbottom trousers and, for some reason, a straw hat. He held a .45 automatic in each hand.

"Don't think I'm trying to find fault, but it's too early in the year for a straw hat," said Cole.

"Up with the hands, smart guy."

Cole obliged.

Carefully stuffing one of the automatics in a coat pocket, Straw-hat frisked Cole.

The boatyard covered several rundown acres. It

was mostly weeds intermingled with a few weathered piles of lumber and a few decayed sheds.

"Would you be the watchman?" asked Cole when the gunman had completed his search.

"My station in life, palsy-walsy, don't matter." He dug out his second gun. Pointing them both at Cole, jabbing at the air with them, he added, "Walk down toward the water, now."

There was a wide opening in the far wall of the fence, where a launching dock may once have stood.

"This is as close to the ocean as I can safely go without getting seasick," said Cole, wondering if Smitty was hearing any of what was going on in here.

"Your friend ain't going to come to your rescue, palsy-walsy," Straw-hat told him. "By now, we got him, too."

Cole said, "Who do you represent, exactly? You look a bit gruff and burly to be a witch."

"It don't make no . . . Hey!"

The planks of the fence over which Cole had climbed began to shake.

Somebody on the other side cried, "Oof!"

The fence shook again, this time starting to splinter.

That distracted Straw-hat.

Cole dived straight at the burly man, low and under the guns. He butted him hard in the lower belly.

"Hey!" repeated Straw-hat.

The force of Cole's charge pushed the gunman back against a pile of rain-warped lumber.

Cole brought both of his hands swinging up, and a fist slammed into each of Straw-hat's armpits.

He dropped one gun, but clung to the other.

Cole pulled on the empty-handed arm, spinning

49

Straw-hat around and slamming him harder into the man-high pile of two-by-fours.

Then Cole caught the gun hand, squeezed the wrist hard.

"Hey!" howled Straw-hat.

"Your vocabulary has diminished sadly, palsy-walsy." Cole increased the pressure on the gunman's wrist.

"Okay, okay." Straw-hat dropped the second gun.

Cole kicked at the gun, to get it out of the way. The ground was muddy here; his foot slipped. He slid, stumbled.

Straw-hat threw a punch into Cole's chin.

When Cole went down on one knee, the gunman didn't try to hit him again. Instead, he grabbed a board off the top of the pile. "Just as soon finish you here, smart guy, as any place."

Cole had regained his balance. He made a try for the fallen automatic.

Straw-hat swung the board like a baseball bat.

Its end dug into Cole's ribs. He went swooping back into the lumber pile.

Straw-hat stalked in on him, the board raised for another crack.

The fence exploded into slivers and chunks of wood. Smitty came smashing through.

"Hey, you!" warned Smitty. "Lay off my buddy."

Straw-hat turned and sent the board flying at Smitty.

The giant sidestepped it.

Cole tried to hold onto the tumble of boards, trying to get his breath back, but he lost his balance and fell on his backside on the ground.

Smitty slowed and let Straw-hat get a good running start for the water. "You okay?" he asked the gasping Cole.

Cole waved a hand at the retreating gunman. "Catch him," he tried to say.

The giant got hold of him under the arms, lifted him to his feet. "I'll prop you up here, Cole."

Before Smitty could take off after Straw-hat, an engine started up at the water's edge. Seconds later, a motor launch was cutting across the gray water.

"Lost him," gasped Cole.

Smitty walked a few feet away and picked up something from the ground. "He left his skimmer behind," he said, spinning the straw-hat around on his finger.

"What about . . . the guys who jumped you?"

"They ran off," said Smitty. "I tossed them into the fence a few times, and it seemed to discourage them. I figured I'd better come in and see about you before I took off after them."

"Quite a . . . dramatic entrance, old chum. Right through . . . the fence."

The giant shrugged modestly. "The wood's old and not too strong," he said. "I could have climbed over, but . . ." He shrugged again.

Cole, taking a wheezing breath, lifted the straw hat off Smitty's fingers. "So we don't have the hoodlums," he said, "and we don't have Miss Barley."

"We ain't got Mac, either."

"This is a setback," admitted Cole, fanning himself with the straw hat. "I'm pretty sure it's only temporary."

CHAPTER X

A Drive In The Country

Cole reached up to the dangling strip of sticky flypaper and rescued the fly who was newly entangled there. "Stay away from places like that," he said. He was in a dim corner of Nightwitch's largest general store, using the wall phone.

"Out-of-town gentleman, I'll bet," Hulda Dolittle, the operator, was saying.

"You're very perceptive, miss," said Cole. "And judging from your voice, quite charming. And now if you could connect me with Gil Lunden's office."

After giggling, the operator put through his call.

"Attorney Lunden's office," answered a young girl.

"I'd like very much to talk to Mr. Lunden."

"Mr. Lunden is not in at the moment. May I take a message?"

"This is rather important. Can you tell me where I might find him?"

"Well . . . I don't know, sir."

"Would he still be out at the widow Waxman's?"

"Well, yes . . . but I don't—"

"Thank you." Cole broke the connection.

"Want me to ring Mrs. Waxman for you?" asked the operator.

"That's positively uncanny, the way you read my mind."

After talking to a housekeeper and to Mrs. Waxman herself, Cole got through to the lawyer.

"Something about Anne?" asked Gil Lunden anxiously.

"We're trying to locate her," said Cole. "I thought perhaps—"

"Isn't she at the paper?"

"No, she's not."

Gil asked, "You're with some law enforcement agency?"

"In a sense. We work for Justice, Inc.," said Cole. "Is there someplace we could meet and talk?"

"Anne can't be missing, too. This is . . . all right, Wilson, I'll be finished here in about a half-hour," he said. "The trouble is I have a meeting later on over in Wickford Point. Do you suppose you could drive out this way? I could meet you at the Old Fiddler's Inn."

"Sounds like a workable plan. How do we get there?"

Gil gave him instructions.

Smitty was leaning on the porch railing outside. "Prewar jawbreakers," he said as he crunched a mouthful of hard candy. He held a small white paper bag clenched in one big fist.

"I talked to Hollis at the newspaper," said Cole, "and thereafter to Anne Barley's inamarato. Her present whereabouts remain a mystery, but the lawyer wants to talk to us. We may learn something."

"We better learn *something* pretty darn quick," said the giant.

Cole balanced the straw hat on his knee, spinning it around, slowly. "Now if I were Sherlock Holmes or Dr. Thorndyke, I'd be able to scrutinize this chapeau and tell you a great deal about our stubby boatyard friend," he remarked. "What he does for a living, his hobbies, his favorite vegetable, and even . . . oh-ho!"

Smitty, who was driving, took his eyes off the country road for a few seconds. "What?"

"My assailant stuffed some paper into the inside hatband to make this thing fit his thick head." Cole extracted several small folded pieces of cardboard from inside the hat. "Not as impressive as pulling out rabbits, but perhaps more informative."

"What's old hunks of waste paper going to tell us?"

Carefully unfolding one of the cards, the grinning Cole said, "One never knows, as Fats Waller oft reminds us. Hum . . . ah . . . hum."

"What, something?"

"For some reason, all these hunks of paper have *With Deepest Sympathy* printed across the top," Cole pointed out. "Either our aggressive chum has a morbid streak, or he's been someplace where they had a stack of these little sympathy cards."

"A florist, maybe?" suggested Smitty. "Or maybe even an undertaking parlor."

Cole deposited one of the cards in the inside pocket of his sportcoat. "We'll look into it."

"Could be the guy bought the lid second-hand."

"Let's look on the bright side, Smitty, and consider this a clue."

They were traveling along a quiet stretch of road; a few farms showed on the distant hills.

"There's the crossroads up ahead," noticed Smitty.

They turned to the right and began climbing the road that would take them to the Old Fiddler's Inn and their meeting with Gil Lunden.

"Must be some horses around here," said Cole after a few moments. "That's a wagon load of hay bales up ahead."

"How about that? A horse-drawn wagon," said Smitty. "That's a nice New England touch."

"Also slow," said Cole. "But I don't think we've got enough room to pass him."

"Maybe I can . . . Damn!" His big foot slammed the brake pedal.

The bales of hay were suddenly toppling off the wagon, bouncing on the road.

"A rural obstacle course," mumbled Cole, holding tight to his seat.

Their car slewed across the road, turning sideways.

Smitty let out his breath. "Didn't hit any of them, anyway."

A dozen large bales of dirty-gold hay dotted the road, blocking their way.

The wagon itself had stopped.

"Might as well be good chaps," said Cole, reaching for the door handle, "and help them reload. We're not going to get to the Old Fiddler until—"

"Back of us," said Smitty, who had glanced into the rear-view mirror.

A green truck had come up behind them and parked sideways. They were effectively bottled in.

Before Cole could comment further, a slug smacked into their windshield, making spiderweb patterns across the glass.

CHAPTER XI

Underground

Rain had started again, but none of it got into the crypt. MacMurdie heard it slapping down on the marble-domed roof as he tried to discover the secret of the hidden doorway.

He'd pushed at the section of wall beneath which the muddy footprints ran, twisted the copper lamps. He had found two hair-thin cracks that ran from floor to ceiling, indicating the section of wall did indeed serve as a door. Nothing he'd tried, so far, had made it open.

"Ye'd better solve this riddle soon," he admonished himself, "or you'll end up making this tomb your permanent home."

He bent and studied once more the footprint trails. The majority of them passed through the wall at the same point.

"Aye, and what do I see here?"

Mac noticed now that some of the footprints, the complete ones, changed in appearance close to the wall. The heel sections were fainter, the ball of the foot looked as though it had widened and pressed down harder.

" 'Twould seem the skurlies hunkered down right about here."

Carefully fitting his own feet into the newest set of prints, the Scot squatted. At eye level he could make out faint smudges on the marble. Mac pressed his fingertips against the two darkest smudges.

Nothing happened.

He pressed harder. The wall began to make a grumbling sound. Mac leaped back as it swung open toward him.

There was a tunnel on the other side. MacMurdie had been hoping for daylight, but at least this was a way out of the crypt.

He crossed the threshold of the shadowy tunnel. When he had traveled twenty feet, the marble wall pivoted shut behind him. There was thick, musty darkness all around him.

Holding out one hand, he made his way over to one wall of the black tunnel. He placed his palm flat against the rock surface and continued his progress forward.

"Getting farther from the light of day step by step."

When he'd traveled another hundred paces, MacMurdie put his other hand out in front of him. He sensed he was coming to some kind of obstruction.

It was a wooden door. Mac located the doorknob and very slowly turned it. The door, with a faint creaking, opened inward.

There was light on the other side, coming from a dangling 100-watt bulb.

There was also a man with a gun.

Gil Lunden set the pewter ale mug down on the bar, glancing again toward the door of the small beam-ceilinged inn tavern.

"More rain," observed the fat old man behind the bar counter. "We haven't had such a wet spring since before the war."

The young attorney nodded as he checked his watch.

"Your friends a mite late?"

Yes, they certainly were. Standing up, Gil said, "In case a Mr. Wilson comes in, tell him I went out to look for him."

He strode to the door, trotted over to his car, and got in. He didn't know what Wilson looked like, or what kind of automobile he was driving, but he thought he'd better go looking for him. There was a possibility he'd taken a wrong turning at the crossroads.

"A strange car, maybe out-of-state, shouldn't be too tough to spot."

As he drove away from the Old Fiddler's Inn, Gil thought about Anne. Mrs. Waxman, with her complaints and the infinite little changes she was considering for her latest will, had rattled him. "Should have gotten more information out of Wilson," he told himself.

Still, maybe he was worrying about nothing. Anne was pretty damn independent. It could be she'd simply gone off to dig into some story and not bothered to tell anybody. That was one of the things he liked about her, her independent approach to things. Sometimes, though, he thought it might be better if she were a little more dependent, on him, anyway.

"She's all right," he said to himself. "You're letting all this talk about witches and warlocks get to you."

You couldn't deny the fact, however, that Dr. Ruyle had disappeared. And, apparently, this fellow MacMurdie, whoever he was.

"What was that outfit Anne said he worked for?"

The rain was coming harder, almost too much for the worn windshield wipers.

"Oh, yeah, Justice, Inc. I heard something about them, read an article somewhere. Wait a minute . . . that's the crime-fighting group headed up by this fellow they call the Avenger."

The attorney shook his head. It all sounded too melodramatic. Especially for a quiet one-horse sort of place like Nightwitch. Witches, sorcerers, the Devil, and now the Avenger.

"Everyday people, and I'm sure as heck one of those, don't get mixed up with such things," Gil told himself as he scanned the road for some sign of Wilson's car.

"One of the reasons I've stayed here is that Nightwitch is such a peaceful place. Even since the war started, not much of that has touched us. It's not as—"

A large hay wagon blocked his progress.

Gil rolled down his window to get a better look at the obstruction.

That was when he heard the gunshots.

CHAPTER XII

Roadwork

"I suppose this is good exercise," said Cole Wilson, diving behind a maple tree.

A bullet came whistling up through the rain. The slug thunked into the bole of a maple tree.

"Maybe we'll get some maple syrup for our troubles," Cole said, "if these chaps keep drilling holes."

Smitty was hunched behind another wide maple. "We should be able to hold off those bozos from here."

Cole and the giant had managed to get clear of their car and hightail it for this wooded hillside before the surrounding gunmen had reached them.

Another slug bit into a tree.

"How many of these rascals do you calculate there are, Smitty?"

"I counted at least five while we was hotfooting it up here."

"Five, or possibly six, to two," reflected Cole. "That's not bad odds." He eased a revolver out of a shoulder holster. "In a way, I regret that I'm not wearing my bullet-proof vest, but when spring approaches I always take the thing off."

"Don't worry, they ain't going to get close enough to nail you."

A bullet whizzed by, chattering through the branches overhead.

"This witch cult," said Cole, "is unlike any other I've ever heard of or encountered." He popped out from his protective tree for a few seconds, long enough to squeeze off a shot.

Downhill, someone howled in pain.

"You got one," announced Smitty. He fished a handful of glass pellets out of his pocket.

"Four, or possibly five, to go," said Cole, grinning. "I always expect—to return to my earlier remarks—witches to be wizened old ladies who ride around on broomsticks and cackle. This bunch seems, so far, to have a membership made up exclusively of heavies with guns."

"Dick's probably right about them being into something else besides mumbo-jumbo, like maybe espionage."

Cole bobbed into the clear for another shot.

This one felled no one.

He said, safe behind the tree, "I'm growing increasingly curious about how they've been able to lay these traps for us."

"Yeah, they sure know everywhere we're going," said the giant.

"Very few people knew we were en route to the picturesque Old Fiddler's Inn."

"Nobody but the legal guy." Smitty flattened out

on the mossy ground. "Keep diverting those mugs, Cole. I'm going to try a little something."

Cole grinned at the giant and flashed from behind his tree to fire again at the stalking gunmen.

Three slugs came whispering up in his direction. One dug into the trunk of his tree, but none hit him.

Smitty, though a huge man, was able to move as stealthily as a jungle cat. He worked his way downhill now, making no sound.

Two of the gunmen were crouched at the lower edge of the woodland area, shielded by a high mound of rocks and boulders. Two others were already in among the trees, intending, probably, to sneak up on the Justice, Inc., teammates.

There might be, for all Smitty knew, even more armed men around than he'd been able to spot. He'd have to take a chance on that.

Up above him, Cole was carrying on a conversation, giving the impression that they were both still up there. ". . . can't see how you prefer the work of Amy Lowell to that of Emily Dickinson, Smitty. Take the question of imagery alone, why . . ."

The giant was only a few yards from the two men behind the rocks.

"What say we charge them?" said one, a porky fellow in a checkered overcoat.

"Charge them?" asked his associate, a tiny hairless man. "This ain't up front, Patsy."

"You don't have to rub it in I'm 4F, Nat. I feel lousy enough without you—"

"I don't care if you're 4F or 1A or 26Q," said the hairless Nat. "I just don't want to go charging up there into the woods. They already winged Willy."

"We could sit here all day and get sopping wet," complained Patsy. "And pretty soon some rube is going to come along the road and raise a squawk about that hay wagon."

"Relax, Charley and Bert will of snuck up on them by then."

Smitty rose up and, taking careful aim, flung one of the glass pellets.

It landed on a rock near Patsy's feet. "Hey!" he exclaimed.

Before either of them could do anything a cloud of blackness enfolded them. The gas in the pellet mixed swiftly with air to produce a nightlike pall which covered several square feet to a height taller than the tallest of the gunmen.

Smitty dived right into the black cloud. In his mind's eye he saw the men as they had been standing at the instant he threw the pellet. Reaching out, he grabbed.

And got his huge fingers around the throat of the hairless Nat.

"Jeeze, it's—"

Smitty applied pressure to a nerve in the little gunman's neck, and he passed out.

The giant went for Patsy.

But Patsy wasn't where he was supposed to be.

Smitty got hold of nothing but black air. Then a bullet zinged by his head.

"Got you now," said Smitty to himself. He hunched low, made a flying tackle.

He was right. He got Patsy around the knees and brought him down, hard, to the ground.

Before the porky gunman could use his gun again, Smitty knocked him out with two short, intense, jabs to the chin.

Very carefully he began to circle the rocks. He didn't know what he'd meet when he stepped out of the black cloud.

There was gunfire up in the woods.

The giant dashed out into clear air. Shielding his eyes from the hard-driving rain, he looked uphill.

There was no sign of anyone up there.

Head tucked down, Smitty went charging up through the pines and maples.

"All clear," said Cole, emerging into view from behind a tree.

"What's up?"

"A couple of them were sneaking up on me, as you may have noticed," explained Cole. "Believing as I do that turnabout is fairplay, I decided to sneak up on them. I succeeded and, having the element of surprise on my side, got a shot at both of them. But instead of sticking around to do combat, they both took off." He pointed to the right. "They are, as Josh so aptly puts it, long gone."

"That's okay," said the big man. "I got us two more down there."

The black cloud was thinning some, but it still masked the two fallen gunmen.

"Let us gather them up, then," suggested Cole.

He and the giant made their way to the mound of rocks.

"You take the little one," said Smitty when they were inside the black pall.

"Which one is that?"

"Well, I got hold of the big one. So whoever you find lying around, you take."

Cole came out of the blackness first. "As soon as this lad comes to his senses, we can ask him what—"

"Holy mackerel!" said Smitty, dropping Patsy beside Nat.

Both men were dead. Each had had his throat cut.

Scanning the area, Smitty said, "Who did it?"

65

"One of the ones who was still alive, obviously."

"Yeah, but I was only up here with you a few minutes."

"They may have had an extra man backing them up."

"Why kill these birds, though?"

"They probably would have preferred to do us in, Smitty. But we looked too formidable," said Cole. "So they did the next best thing, and silenced these poor chaps."

"This is more than witchcraft," said Smitty. "They wanted these guys quiet for some other reason."

"Never underestimate the power of the Devil," said Cole.

A car door slammed down the road. A young man got out and waved. "Say, would one of you be Wilson?"

"Indeed one of us would," Cole called back.

"I'm Gil Lunden," he said. "I got worried and came looking for you."

"I was worried there for a while myself." Cole went over to the muddy road to him.

CHAPTER XIII

Dr. Winters On The Case

The auto was impressive—long and low, glistening black, so highly polished that the rain beaded on its bright surface. It appeared before the Colonial Inn late in the afternoon.

One of Nightwitch's elder citizens was standing under the awning, watching the rain splash in the puddles on the sidewalk. He'd been trying to whittle an alder branch, but he was a little shaky as a result of sampling some bad applejack last night. He watched the handsome car, noticing it was driven by a young woman—a right pretty young girl, with blond hair.

The rear door of the auto opened, and a young man in a tweed suit, with a rumpled raincoat over his shoulders, hopped out. He was carrying a fat briefcase and several thick books. He hurried up the steps of the inn, then halted and looked back. "Ah, Miss Spaulding, I neglected to wait for you. Forgive me, I was thinking of . . . something else."

The diminutive blonde smiled pleasantly as she climbed out through the rain to join him. "Think nothing of it, Dr. Winters." She, too, was loaded down with a briefcase and a stack of old books.

They went inside. The old man returned to watching the rain fall.

The small clerk was resting in one of the big chairs in the lobby. He got to his feet as the Avenger and Nellie Gray arrived. "Yes?"

"I'm . . ." began Benson, pausing to stroke his chin. "Ah, yes, I'm Dr. Montague Winters. Perhaps you've heard of me?"

Moving behind his desk, the clerk said, "Well, sir, I know your secretary phoned in a reservation early this morning. Miss Spaulding, isn't it?"

Nellie smiled at him. "Yes, you have a very good memory."

"You more or less have to, in this business." He tugged out a drawer, fingered through a pile of papers and cards. "Yes, here's the reservation. A room for Dr. Montague Winters and a room for his secretary Miss Emmy Lou Spaulding. I put you folks in 101 and 102, up on the second floor. If that suits you?"

Benson had wandered off and was squinting at a primitive portrait that hung over the fireplace. "Excellent piece of work, exceptional," he murmured.

"That your line of work, pictures and such?" asked the clerk as he passed the register across the counter toward Nellie.

The Avenger turned. "I can see you haven't heard

of me," he said. "I suppose that's to be expected. No, my field of interest is . . . witchcraft."

The clerk blinked, swallowed. "Witchcraft?"

Walking toward him, Benson continued, "Surely you know, a man immersed in the relics of the past as you are, that this town was once the center of a practicing coven of witches and warlocks?"

"Oh, you mean back in the old days," said the clerk, after licking his lips. "Yes, that's certainly true, professor. Yes, a good many strange things went on back then, so legend has it."

"Exactly," said Benson. "Which explains my being here. I am researching a book on the witchcraft of New England. You may have seen my earlier work, *Devils and Demons of Middle Europe.*"

"I don't do much reading," admitted the clerk. "When I do, I usually buy a few of these pulp magazines over to Gibson's General Store."

"I see, I see."

"Perhaps we'd better get up to our rooms, professor," suggested Nellie. "We've had a long drive over from Princeton, and in your condition . . ."

"Yes, yes, I suppose you're right."

The clerk located two keys and led them up a shadowy darkwood staircase to their rooms.

The man with the gun was tall, very blond. He gestured with the .38 revolver in his hand. "Step along this way, Mr. MacMurdie." A faint trace of accent was noticeable in his speech.

"Would ye be a paid-up member of the coven, lad?"

"That needn't concern you," the blond man said. "It was a mistake to have stashed you up in the

69

crypt. Very clever of you to have discovered a way out."

"The wrong way, it seems."

The blond man said, "You will walk along this corridor now, if you please."

Mac complied with the gunman's order.

"Unfortunately for you, Mr. MacMurdie, every time the door in the crypt opens, a light flashes down here," said the blond man. "That's far enough. Stop by that wall lamp there, please."

Mac glanced around at the wooden walls and at the beams that supported the low ceiling. "Where mot we be?"

"It really doesn't matter." Keeping the revolver trained on the Scot, he reached up and twisted the base of the lamp.

"These walls are nae new," observed Mac.

A section of the wood paneling slid, jerkingly, aside. There was a heavy metal door behind that.

The gunman pressed several spots on the door, and it grated open. He gave MacMurdie a sharp push, his hand slamming hard between the shoulder blades.

Mac went stumbling forward into darkness.

The floor was slanted. He couldn't keep himself from moving ahead. He grabbed out, but couldn't get hold of anything but darkness.

Chill air hit him, and then he was falling. Down and down.

CHAPTER XIV

Captives

Anne Barley sneezed.

There was dust lying thick on most of the surfaces of the dim room she had found herself in. It was a stone-walled room, with an ancient wooden table against one wall and an equally antique chair in its center. The only light came from a weak wire-shielded bulb in the ceiling.

Anne had awakened a few minutes earlier. The lower part of her face felt vaguely strange; her lips and nostrils burned. She remembered they'd pressed something over her face. They'd grabbed her from behind, down at the old dock area where she'd been trying to find some trace of a boat accident.

And now she was here. When Anne left the chair, she discovered she couldn't quite walk steadily yet. She kept at it, though, determined to explore the entire room.

71

After a few moments she said, "I'm starting to feel like one of those ships in a bottle. I know I'm in here, but I can't see how they did it."

She could discover no trace of a doorway.

"They popped me in here, so there's got to be a way to get out."

Anne climbed up onto the rickety chair and studied the stone ceiling of her cell.

She was still up there when a section of the far wall swung open. She turned, then laughed. "Sam, thank goodness! I don't know how you found me, but . . ." The look on her editor's face made her stop talking all at once. "Sam?"

There was a smile on Sam Hollis's gaunt face, a twisted, unsettling smile. "I really can't blame you, Anne," he said. "You're a pretty fair reporter, and any good reporter is going to dig once he smells a story. I wish, though, you'd kept out of this one."

"Oh, Sam." She climbed to the floor, sank into the chair. "You mean you . . . you're one of them?"

Nodding, the rawboned man approached closer. "Yes, that's right," he answered. "You kept this story to yourself, mostly. Too bad, because if I'd known what you were up to a little sooner, I might have been able to steer you off the trail. Now, though, you're too involved."

"It's not only me, Sam," she reminded him. "It's Dr. Ruyle and Mr. MacMurdie. If you harm them . . . you're going to have to contend with Justice, Inc. I don't know if you know who—"

"I know all about Justice, Inc., Anne. And about this self-styled Avenger," cut in Hollis. "We can handle any of them, the same way we handled MacMurdie."

"You did something to him . . . what did you do?"

72

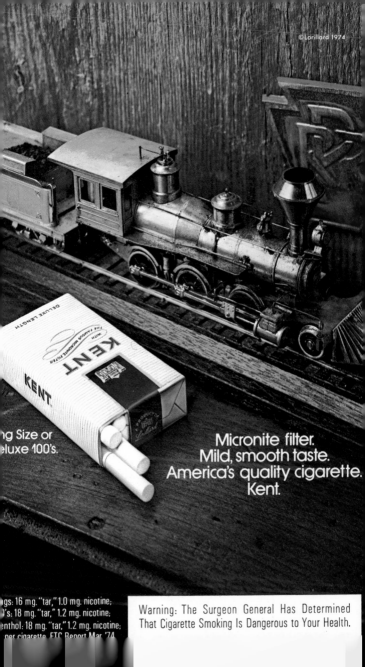

©Lorillard 1974

DELUXE LENGTH

KENT

KENT

ng Size or
luxe 100's.

Micronite filter.
Mild, smooth taste.
America's quality cigarette.
Kent.

gs: 16 mg. "tar," 1.0 mg. nicotine;
's: 18 mg. "tar," 1.2 mg. nicotine;
enthol: 18 mg. "tar," 1.2 mg. nicotine;
per cigarette FTC Report Mar '74

Try the crisp, clean taste of Kent Menthol.

The only Menthol with the famous Micronite filter.

Kings: 16 mg. "tar," 1.0 mg. nicotine;
100's: 18 mg. "tar," 1.2 mg. nicotine;
Menthol: 18 mg. "tar," 1.2 mg. nicotine;
av. per cigarette, FTC Report Mar. '74.

"He came spying on a meeting, no doubt because of a tip you kindly supplied him," answered Hollis. "We have him now, here."

Shivering against her will, Anne asked, "Where is this place? Where are we?"

"You didn't do enough digging into the background of Nightwitch, girl. I know, you were concentrating on the witch lore," said the editor, chuckling. "In the last century, after the bay ceased to be an active port, there was quite a profitable smuggling trade carried on here. They were very ambitious in those days, and labor was cheap. So a series of tunnels and storerooms were built underground. The system links up with the harbor and also with the old Bald Hill Cemetery. It's proved to be quite handy."

"The witchcraft, then," said the girl, "that's not the important thing at all, is it?"

Hollis chuckled. "It's important to most of the fools who have joined the cult, the female witches and the male warlocks. To them, people who yearn for the simple solutions of a bygone time, it is highly important."

"But not to you, Sam, you don't believe any of it."

"I believe in the job I was sent here to do," he answered. "Sent here nearly ten years ago to prepare for."

Slowly, Anne nodded her head. "You're a spy."

"Much more than that, Anne. I'm an agent, an agent of change, a representative of the winning ideology in the world," he said.

"And the meetings of the witch cult, that's only a cover."

"Most of the fools in the coven do not know that," replied Hollis. "I did a great deal of research into the history of this community. I learned, as I told you, about this magnificent system of underground tunnels—something no one else in Nightwitch even realizes the existence of. I also discovered that a witch cult flourished here in the late seventeenth century. Now, I know these people, Anne. They're simple, a lot of them, superstitious. I calculated that a witch group could be started up again, if it was handled just right."

"You use it to cover the activities of your spies," said Anne.

"For much more than that," Hollis said, chuckling. "You see, Anne, we're landing agents here in the harbor. It's a tricky business, but we've been highly successful so far. With a witch cult going strong, well, a good many people are going to stay home at night. And they're not going to report a couple of cloaked, muffled figures they might see on a back road. It's worked very well."

"Until now," she told him.

"You're only a very small annoyance, not a setback."

"What do you expect to do with me, Sam, keep me a prisoner forever?"

"Oh, no, Anne, I have something much more interesting planned for you," he answered. "I've been preparing my fold for something like this for a long time, just in case we had to get rid of a meddler."

"Preparing them for what?"

"A human sacrifice," he said.

MacMurdie landed, after a drop of what felt like six or seven feet, on a stone floor.

"What is it?" called out a voice in the blackness. "What's that?"

" 'Tis Fergus MacMurdie, feeling none too bright."

"Mac!" said John Ruyle. "It's me, John."

"Ah, 'tis happy I am to find ye're alive and kicking."

"Alive, at least," said his friend. "Do you have any idea, Mac, what's going on?"

"Aye, I've got a few," replied the Scot.

"I mean, where are we exactly?"

" 'Twould be my guess there's some sort of underground passageway system been built beneath one of your old burying grounds or kirkyards. These birkies are using it for their own purposes."

"I thought I knew what their purposes were, Mac," said Ruyle in the absolute dark. "Now, I've been thinking all the time I've been down here, I'm not as sure."

"The witches," said Mac, "are only part of it."

"Yes, that's what I concluded. But what else are they up to?"

"We have to get out of here," said Mac, "and find out just that."

CHAPTER XV

Famous Last Words

Nellie knocked on the connecting door, then stepped into the Avenger's room. "Everybody," she announced, "seems to be elsewhere."

Benson had been sitting, fingers peaked beneath his jaw, in a chair by the window. Heavy rain pattered on the glass behind his head. "Where?"

The little blonde crossed the flowered rug. "This is a small, somewhat old-fashioned, town," she said. "They've got their secrets, of course, but everybody seems to know a heck of a lot about what everyone else is up to. The desk clerk told me, when I tried to call Mac's room, that nobody's seen him since last night." She frowned. "He says the police are looking into it."

"The police?" Benson stood up. "Why?"

"Apparently the clerk got worried," explained Nellie. "Some gent who does odd jobs for the inn saw Mac leap out of his room last night at the witching hour. Clerk says all sorts of people have been asking for Mac, so he decided maybe he was missing."

"Who was asking for him, besides Cole and Smitty?"

Sitting on the edge of the four-poster bed, Nellie took out a notebook from her purse. She flipped it open and read to the Avenger what the clerk had told her about Anne Barley and about the arrival of Cole and Smitty. She slammed the book shut, adding, "The chief of police let Cole and Smitty poke around Mac's room, but they didn't find anything. Right now, Cole and our resident giant are out looking for this Barley girl. Which is what you'd expect Cole to be doing."

"I wonder," said the Avenger, "how long I can go on posing as an absent-minded scholar here to do a paper on the witch trials of the seventeenth century?"

Nellie glanced at her tiny wristwatch. "I'd give it another two hours," she said. "As I told you, the people around here seem to know what you're up to before you do. I imagine half of Nightwitch is gossiping about us right now."

"I'm convinced, which is why I decided to come here myself, that Mac's witches tie in with the rise of sabotage in this area," he said. "So we've got to . . ." He took hold of the minature sending and receiving set built into the buckle of his belt. "I'm going to try and see if I can contact them. We'll try for Mac first."

Benson sent out a signal that only MacMurdie's set would receive. He tried several times, but there was no response.

"Nothing from Mac at all." The Avenger shook

77

his head, frowning. "Now let's see about Cole and Smitty."

But those signals drew no response, either.

The reason for that is simple. We'll have to go back an hour to find out why.

The printer was extremely old, smeared with black ink and flecks of snuff. After Cole had been talking to him for several minutes, he leaned forward in his desk chair. "Maybe, young feller, I ought to tell you I'm a mite deaf."

Cole halted, grinning. "I'm glad you have," he said. "How much have you heard so far?"

"That's right, deaf."

Holding the sympathy card he'd found inside the gunman's straw hat, Cole shouted. "Did you print this?"

"Yep," said the ancient printer.

"For who?"

"Yep, I printed it."

Smitty decided to try a bellow. "For whom?"

The old man started. "No need to scream, I ain't stone deaf." He tottered up out of his chair. "Just let me check my records."

They followed him through the labyrinth of twisting corridors and workrooms that made up his ancient printshop.

"Look at there," said the printer. "Another darn leak in the roof."

Rain was gurgling in through a dollar-size hole in the ceiling, splashing on top of several rusty filing cabinets.

"Don't fret," said the old man, "the records you want ain't in that part of the storeroom. Yessir, here we are." He clutched at the handle of a green drawer. Nothing happened. "Dang thing always did stick."

Smitty pulled the reluctant drawer out. "There you go."

"Now, that type on that particular card was something they called Busino Extra Lite. Never caught on, and it was give up back before the war."

"This war?" asked Cole.

"No, no, the Great War, back in 'Eighteen. This war, he says." After some digging into the faded file folders, the printer produced a slip of pink paper. "Here it is. I thought I remembered that job. Run off five thousand of them little cards for the Bald Hill Floral Shoppe. See, right here. Five thousand cards incribed *With Deepest Sympathy,* set in 10-point Busino Extra Lite. Yep, picked up on April 5, 1917."

"That's over twenty-five years ago," observed Cole.

"Told you they don't use that typeface no more."

"Whereabouts," asked Smitty, "is this Bald Hill Floral outfit?"

"No place."

"No place?"

"They went bust first year of the Depression, even before that fellow Roosevelt took over the country."

"Where were they located back then?" Cole asked him.

"Well, where do you think? Right across the road from the Bald Hill cemetery."

"I should have guessed," grinned Cole.

"You can have it," remarked Smitty.

"Ah, what's become of your usual Pollyanna side?" asked Cole as the giant parked alongside the tumble-down wrought-iron fence on their left. "Here's a lovely weed-infested cemetery, which no

79

one has obviously entered, dead or alive, since the reign of Hoover I. Here is this ragtag graveyard full of cracked tombstones and toppled markers being battered with a torrential downfall of rain, and you say it gives you the creeps."

"That flower shop we just drove by don't look so jolly, either."

"It does, however, look like the sort of place a gang of hoodlums and bravos might use as a hangout."

"Could be." The big man set the brake. "We're out of sight of the joint, so let's mosey back through that woods across the way for a look-see."

"Very well, if you're through admiring the gothic splendor of Bald Hill Cemetery proper." Cole left the car, pulling down the brim of his hat and turning up the collar of his coat.

The two Justice, Inc., teammates sprinted across the road and into the wooded area. Soon they were weaving their way toward the building which once had housed the flower shop. The heavy rain came zigzagging down through the twists of branches.

Smitty, who was in the lead, held out his hand. "Whoa, there she is." He stopped behind a tree trunk, nodding at the building.

Rainwater was cascading down across the slanting tile roof, splashing into a greenish water barrel. The windows were boarded up, the rear door chained and padlocked.

"Don't look like they been open for business in a while," said the giant.

"Camouflage," said Cole. "If you'll cast an eye on the path leading up to the door, you'll notice the still-visible scrape mark made when that door was recently opened. Also, look there, you'll find mud on the bottom of the door from said scrape."

"Hard to be sure, with the rain slopping mud every which way."

"I'm sure," said Cole. "Somebody's using that building, and the odds are they're in there right now."

"Not all of them," said a voice behind them.

It was Straw-hat, minus his straw hat, but carrying two automatics.

"We're interested in a floral piece made in the shape of a bass fiddle, to be sent to my late uncle who—"

"Once again," said the gunman, "I suggest you put up your hands. Then I'd like you to step into the office over there."

"You sure move quiet," commented Smitty. "We never even heard you."

"Yeah, I'm pretty good at—"

While Straw-hat had been turned toward Smitty to explain his stalking ability, Cole had jumped into action. He swung out, flat-handed, and dealt the gunman a chop against the side of the neck.

Gagging, the man began to sway.

As Straw-hat bumped into the trunk of the nearest tree, a tiny buzzing sounded in Cole's belt radio. He ignored the signal and knocked one of the man's guns away.

"More coming," warned Smitty.

Three men, each wearing a yellow slicker and two carrying shotguns, had come running around the side of the stone building.

Smitty bent to grab up the .45 automatic that Straw-hat had dropped.

81

Unexpectedly, as Cole struggled to take the other gun away, Straw-hat kicked out with one booted foot.

"Hey!" The toe of the heavy boot nudged hard into the side of Smitty's head. He let go the automatic and sloshed to one knee in the muddy ground.

"Hold it right there, big boy!" shouted the closest man with a shotgun. He was now only ten feet from them. "Stay down on your knees, or you'll get your noggin blowed clean off."

Cole succeeded in wresting the second automatic from Straw-hat. He waited an instant, then gave the man a tremendous shove in the direction of the aproaching trio.

Straw-hat went dancing across the mud, flapping his arms to keep his balance, his booted feet kicking up slushy mud.

Cole grabbed Smitty's arm. "Come on, let's make a hasty departure."

The big man put his hand to his head. "I can't seem to . . ." All expression left his face. He dropped forward.

Cole left him and ran. Stopping with a tree trunk at his back, he tugged out his belt-buckle radio. "Bald Hill Floral Shoppe," he said into the receiver. "Bald Hill Floral Shoppe. We got trouble."

Then they were on him.

CHAPTER XVI

The Avenger Takes A Hand

Late in the afternoon the rain slackened. The sky lightened slightly, turning from a chalky gray to a muddy brown. The old panel truck came bouncing along the road, only one windshield wiper working. Lettered on its side was Crittenden Bros. Wholesale Flowers. With a rattle and a cough of smoke, the venerable vehicle turned off the road and came to a stop near the front door of the defunct Bald Hill Floral Shoppe.

A medium-sized young man bounded out of the driver's seat and began pounding with his fist on the boarded-over glass door. After doing that for nearly a full minute, he let off. Scratching his head through his checkered cap, he looked anxiously around. Then he tried pounding on the door again.

"Hey, this stuff is perishable," he shouted. "You want me to leave it sitting out here, or what?"

Two more minutes went by. Far off, on the other side of the low hills, thunder started rumbling.

The truck driver squatted, putting his eyes to the keyhole. At the same time he rattled the doorknob. "Wake up in there," he urged. "I got six dozen carnations for you guys."

The front door didn't open, but from around the side of the building came a very thin man in a yellow slicker. "What seems to be the trouble, young man?"

"You the Bald Hill Floral Shoppe?" asked the Avenger.

"Closed for the duration," said the thin man.

"Then why in blazes are you ordering six dozen of our best-quality carnations?"

"We're not, nobody did."

Benson strode back to the cab of his truck, grabbed a clipboard off the front seat. "I got the bill of lading right here and it states—"

"This states you better beat it." A gun, a snubnosed .38 revolver, appeared in his hand. "Whatever you're selling, we don't want any."

"Listen," persisted Benson, "somebody ordered the flowers, and you're going to have to pay for them."

"Don't you hear very well?" The thin man jabbed the gun at the Avenger. "Get in that jalopy and get moving away from here."

"I think not." The Avenger's foot kicked up, connecting with the thin man's gun hand.

"Damn!" The weapon went spinning up out of his grasp.

Before the thin man could do anything beyond lifting his head to watch the gun climb, Benson had taken hold of his throat. The Avenger pressed certain spots in the man's neck.

84

The thin man had no choice. He passed out, fell down onto the muddy gravel.

Taking hold of the unconscious man by the armpits, the Avenger dragged him around to the rear of the panel truck.

Before his hand reached the door handle, another gunman appeared on the scene, wearing also a yellow slicker, running toward him, carrying a shotgun.

"Hey, buddy, what the hell do you think you're doing?"

The Avenger turned to face him. "Collecting," he answered.

"Huh? Collecting what?" He came up to within a couple of feet of the rear of the truck.

"Hoodlums."

"Oh, yeah? Well, you—"

All at once, Benson threw himself to the ground.

The back doors of the truck slammed open. The left-hand one took the shotgun man in the nose, elbow, and knee.

He howled, went flapping back about a dozen feet before falling down on his backside. Muddy water splashed as he sat.

The Avenger scooted over to him, knocked the shotgun out of his hands. "You might as well stay down," he said to the sprawled man.

Two chops to the side of the head accomplished that.

"Reinforcements," warned Nellie, who'd swung the metal doors open into the man's face.

Two more gunmen were trotting around the side of the stone shop. They wasted no time in talk or warnings. They started shooting.

The Avenger wasn't where he had been when the guns were aimed and fired. Neither the slug from

Straw-hat's right-hand automatic nor the scatter of pellets from the other man's shotgun came near him.

Benson kept rolling across the gravel. When he bounded to his feet, there was a weapon in each hand—in his right, the unique pistol he had dubbed Mike, and in his left the exceptional knife he called Ike.

"Drop it," warned Straw-hat, his fingers tightening on the triggers of both automatics.

But even as he spoke, a .22 slug was whizzing from the gun. It deftly creased his skull. Straw-hat dropped.

The knife blade sliced at the other man's hands. He cried out in pain, let go of his shotgun. He slapped at each hand in turn, splashing blood all over the front of his yellow raincoat. The rain swiftly washed it away.

Nellie sprinted over to him, twisted an arm behind his back. "Stand still," she suggested.

"I'm bleeding like a stuck pig, I'm going to bleed to death before your eyes."

"Nonsense," said the blonde. "Okay, I'll let you go. Here, put this handkerchief—leave it folded up—against your hand and press hard with the other one."

"Oh, that's not going to do any good. There's so much blood, I . . ." The man's face paled, turning to a shade of yellow that matched his raincoat. His eyes flapped shut, his mouth fished open, and he slumped to the ground.

"Can't stand the sight of blood," said Nellie. She shrugged, knelt beside him, and bandaged up his moderately gashed hands with two white handkerchiefs.

"They promised us peace and quiet when we took this country place," said Cole Wilson, peering out

86

through the opening front door of the flower shop. "What brings you to Nightwitch, pixie?"

"Is Smitty okay?"

"Yeah, sure, Nell," called the giant. He pushed Cole aside and stepped out into the rain. "A couple hours from now, you maybe would get a different answer."

"These chaps have made some dire threats," said Cole. He waited until the Avenger had retrieved his throwing knife, then held out his hand. "Good to see you, Richard. I see you got my message."

Benson nodded. "Is this the whole bunch, these four?"

"It's all they had holding us," answered Cole. "But these gents are, to coin a phrase, merely the tip of the proverbial iceberg. We're dealing with something big here, Richard."

"I sensed as much," said the Avenger. "What about Mac?"

"He's still alive," said Cole, "from what hints these goons dropped."

"Any idea where he is?"

"Nope," said Smitty. "I ain't sure these bozos even know. Like Cole says, there's a lot of guys involved in this goofy business. I got the idea Mac got grabbed by the witches themselves."

Glancing around at the four sprawled men, the Avenger said, "We'll question each of them."

"We can use the flower shop for interrogations," said Cole. "As my old chum Straw-hat very recently pointed out, it's quiet and secluded here."

CHAPTER XVII

Conference

Straw-hat, it turned out, was the only one who knew anything much.

Using a pellet of truth gas, which he broke beneath the gunman's nose, the Avenger put him into a half-awake state.

He slumped in the sprung old sofa chair he was sitting in, eyes half closing. His crease wound had been treated, and there was a cross-hatch of bandages on his scalp.

"You will answer all my questions," Benson told him, "truthfully."

"Yes, sir."

The rain drummed on the tile roof and ran down the outside of the dirty windows. The thunder rolled closer.

"Who hired you?"

"The Devil."

Nellie, who was sitting cross-legged on a warped counter top taking notes, raised her eyebrows.

The Avenger asked, "What's his name?"

"The Devil, I don't know his real name. Never dealt with him directly."

"How do you get your orders?"

"By phone," answered Straw-hat. "Sometimes by letter. When we get paid off, the dough is left in envelopes at certain places."

Cole frowned, began stroking his chin.

Benson said, "What sort of jobs have you done for the Devil?"

"All sorts of things. Rough up people, swipe certain things, all sorts of odd jobs."

"The Barley girl," put in Cole. "Did you kidnap her?"

"Well, we took her someplace. Knocked her out first, then delivered her."

"Delivered her where?" asked Benson.

"Sort of a funny place. We got orders to leave her in the living room of a deserted house on Blackpond Road. Place called the old McRobb mansion."

Cole leaned closer to the dazed man. "Where did you grab the girl?"

"Down by the boatyard, where we tangled with you."

"How'd you know we'd be showing up there?"

"Got a phone call," replied Straw-hat. "Told us to go back to the boatyard and grab a couple more nosy people."

"Huh," remarked Smitty. "Nobody knew we were going there, except that newshound guy."

89

"Did Sam Hollis phone you?" asked Cole.

"Don't know who called me. Same voice as always, the Devil."

The Avenger took over the questioning once more. "What about MacMurdie?"

"Witches got him."

"Where?"

"Don't know."

"When are they meeting next?"

"Tonight, I think."

"Where?"

"They got a new location, in a big abandoned barn at a place called White Horse Hill," said Straw-hat. "Going to have something special tonight, I heard."

"What?"

"Sacrifice of somebody to Satan," said the man.

"Ah," said Cole, "rain on a tin roof, nothing is cozier, is it, pixie?"

"I can think of several things," replied Nellie. "None of which include you."

The Avenger and the three members of the Justice, Inc., team were seated in the back of the panel truck. Their four prisoners were still inside the old stone building, securely bound. Before turning them over to the local police, the Avenger wished to hold a conference—hold it where the captives would have no chance of overhearing.

"Do you think," asked Nellie, "this gang of witches will go so far as to actually sacrifice someone?"

"They don't sound any too gentle," said Cole.

"We have to operate on the assumption that they will," said Benson. "Therefore, I plan to attend their conclave this evening and see to it no violence is

90

done to anyone." He nodded in the direction of the crouching giant. "You'll come along with me, Smitty."

"Okay," said Smitty. "I'm still thinking about what that guy with the straw hat was saying. How he got a phone call telling him to expect us at the boatyard. Then, when we was driving out to see that mouthpiece, they knew about that, too."

"It begins to look as though," said Cole, "Sam Hollis must have some connection with the witches. However, there is another possibility."

"Like what?"

"I've noticed that the sweet lady who handles the phone service in Nightwitch has a habit of listening in on calls," said Cole. "Granted, it's a common practice in small towns . . . large towns, too, for all I know."

Smitty snapped his big fingers. It made an enormous popping sound. "Sure, she could have heard us set up that meeting with Gil Lunden."

"Another thing struck me as Straw-hat bared his soul," continued Cole. "He implied that many of their nefarious deeds were openly discussed over the telephone. Indeed, the Devil himself called him on occasion. Seems to me that if our Mrs. Dolittle— which diligent inquiries revealed to be the good operator's name—if she heard a chap saying, 'Hello there, Straw-hat, this is your old pal Satan . . .' Well, it might give her pause. And yet witches and warlocks are phoning hoodlums and heavies all over the place, and not a peep has popped out of Mrs. D."

"She's certainly," said the Avenger, "someone we'll check up on."

"What about the house he mentioned?" asked the little blonde. "The McRobb place, where they left

91

the girl. Do you think there's any chance she's still there?"

"No, it was most likely only a drop," said Benson. "But I want you and Cole to go there and search the house."

"Ah, splendid," said the grinning Cole. "You realize that I have yet to meet the girl in the case. It's not like me."

Smitty slapped his knees impatiently. "Okay, we got our jobs figured out," he said. "We better start loading those bozos into the truck. I got a hunch Chief Storm's not going to let us off without a lot of talk."

"He was rather voluble when we turned in that last batch of goons," said Cole.

Smitty glanced at the Avenger, got a nod, and rose up. He hopped out of the truck into the rain.

CHAPTER XVIII

Secret Places

Chief Storm of the Nightwitch police searched through his desk drawers again. This time he found the pipe he was looking for, stuck it between his teeth. Rain pattered on the station windows; water gurgled through a drainpipe just outside. "Nothing," said the chief, "like this has ever happened in Nightwitch."

"Not in this century," said Benson. An hour earlier, they had presented Storm with the thugs, identified themselves to him and, over his startled protests, left. Now, satisfied that the kick to Smitty's head had done no lasting damage, they had returned.

They had told Storm some, but not all, of what they had learned thus far. "Witches," he said, sucking on the stem of his unlit pipe. "Them four rowdies you brought in for me to lock up, they sure aren't witches and warlocks."

"They've simply been working for the cult."

"Witches," repeated Storm. "Well, I have heard a few rumors 'bout something like that. In a town like this, though, you're always hearing rumors."

"These were based on fact."

"I've got to do something, then," said Chief Storm. "Some old-time practices and beliefs I could let be, but not witchcraft."

"I think," said the Avenger, "the cult will cease to be, very shortly."

"You got more information about this than you're giving out."

"Perhaps."

Storm said, "I checked up on you, Benson, I made a few phone calls."

"And what did you learn?"

"That I might as well go along with you, play this thing your way," said Storm.

"By tomorrow," said Benson, "I may have more to tell you."

Nodding, the chief said, "By tomorrow we're probably going to have some government agents hanging around town. You know about that?"

"Yes."

"So this isn't all magic spells and broomsticks."

"It sure as heck ain't," said Smitty.

The darkness turned to light. Then everything was black night again, and thunder shook the trees.

"Nothing to fear, princess," Cole assured Nellie. "They've got a whole collection of lightning rods on yon rooftop."

"Lighting's never scared me," said the little blonde.

The rain was falling hard once again, battering

94

down through the branches that interlaced above their heads.

Taking the girl's arm, Cole guided her through the wooded area that bordered the old McRobb mansion.

Another flash of lightning illuminated the house, which loomed a hundred yards away from them. The mansion was enormous, thick with towers and turrets and spires.

"Sometimes," said Nellie, "I get the distinct impression that Richard Henry Benson doesn't believe in the equality of the sexes."

"I'm sure he knows you're more than equal, pixie."

"This job tonight, for instance. Obviously it's going to be nice and safe," Nellie complained. "All the fun, that's going to be at the witch convention."

Cole grinned. "Don't be pessimistic, Little Nell. We may find untold adventure awaiting us here in this pile of architectural aberrations."

"Dubious," said the girl.

They reached the edge of the woods. A half-acre of tall grass and a great variety of weeds stood between them and the house.

After staring at the place for a moment, Cole said, "No signs of movement, not even a ghostly light."

"Everybody's at the meeting," said Nellie.

"Let's, therefore, be bold and walk right in the front door."

Nellie tugged the hood of her black raincoat tighter around her head. "Race you," she challenged.

The two of them went dashing across the weedy field, pelted by the rain.

The blonde bounded up the wooden front steps a

good ten seconds ahead of Cole. "Listening to you panting," she said.

"Merely subterfuge, pixie," Cole replied. "I allowed you to win, but I wanted you to think it was because I was a bit winded."

"Unlikely," said the girl. With hands on hips she was studying the oaken front door. The brass knocker was in the shape of a lion's head. The huge doorknob also had the likeness of a lion upon it. "Fond of lions, the McRobbs must have been."

Reaching around her, Cole turned the knob. It moved. A gentle shove caused the door to swing silently inward. "Disappointing, no *Inner Sanctum* creaks."

Nellie clicked on the flashlight she'd been carrying in her raincoat pocket. "Look, footprints all over the place."

Along the right-hand side of the long, bare hall several sets of muddy footprints showed.

"That must be the living room where they deposited the girl," said Cole.

The doorway was midway along the hall, masked with heavy draperies. The footprints led straight to it.

Cole walked to it and slowly pulled aside the aged purple draperies. He peered into the room.

Lightning struck outside at that instant, filling the room with pale yellow light. There was no one in there among the shrouded furniture.

"No lost ladies here," remarked Cole.

Nellie shone her flash into the now dark room. "Somebody was in there," she said. "There are tracks in the dust." She crossed the threshold. "And you can see here where someone was dragged across the floor. Dragged right into this wall." The beam of light climbed up the wall from the floor. "You know, a lot of these ancient houses have secret passages, sections of the wall that open into secret places. That could be what we're dealing with here. Yes, it has to be."

The room turned sickly yellow again, then thunder rattled the leaded windows.

"What we have to do," continued Nellie, "is find out how they got this particular wall to open. That shouldn't be too tough for someone with your self-confessed astuteness, should it?"

There was no reply.

"Cole?" Nellie turned toward the doorway, shining her light on the place where Cole had been.

He was no longer there.

CHAPTER XIX

Midnight

Anne Barley recognized the first witch.

The hooded faces of the other two figures who entered her cell she could not make out. The woman in the lead carried an oil lantern aloft; its flickering, smoky light made deep shadow patterns across the faces of the other two.

"You will rise up and come with us," ordered the witch in a dulled voice.

"Hulda? Hulda Dolittle," said Anne. "You're not involved with these maniacs, are you?"

"The hour is at hand." Hulda was a heavyset woman of fifty. Her eyes had a blank look, and her lips barely moved when she spoke.

Anne ran to her, took hold of her shoulders. "Do you know what they're planning to do to me, Hulda? Do you?"

"You will be sacrificed to the Master," droned the witch in reply.

"This isn't the Dark Ages, Hulda. What they're planning, it's murder."

"It is the will of the Master," answered the witch. "It must be done."

Anne spun away, tried to run around the woman and get to the entryway that they had opened in the wall.

The other two hooded figures were men, large powerful men. They both got hold of her, held her tight by the arms.

"Those who have been chosen," Hulda told her as she struggled to pull free, "must obey. There is no escape from the will of Satan, no escape from the Power."

"You're crazy," shouted Anne. "All of you. Let me go."

"You can not escape from that which is ordained," said one of the men who held her.

It was McClennan, the town postmaster.

Anne kicked him, as hard as she could, in the knee.

The man did not react at all. His eyes, too, were glazed and staring. "Come, the hour is at hand."

"For the glory of Satan," said Hulda.

Kicking out again, Anne cried, "Wake up, all of you! Don't you even realize what you're doing?"

"For the glory of Satan," repeated McClennan.

Anne screamed, then cried out. But that did not stop them from carrying her away down a dark stone corridor.

"Hout," exclaimed MacMurdie. "Here 'tis."

"What?" asked Dr. Ruyle in the absolute darkness.

99

" 'Tis a hair-thin crack in this wall," said Mac, slapping at the stone. "Ah, and here's another one right here."

"Some kind of concealed door?"

" 'Twell could be."

Ruyle asked, "Do you think you can open it?"

"Aye, given time." His fingertips made tiny rasping sounds as he moved them over the wall.

After a few quiet moments, Ruyle said, "It's possible, isn't it, that your associates will come searching for you?"

"They should be—some of them at any rate—in Nightwitch by now," answered Mac. "I telephoned Justice, Inc., before I fell into these skurlies' hands."

"You believe these witches are tied in with some kind of espionage, Mac?"

"I do. There's more than a witch cult operating here."

"Perhaps so. I don't know, though, these people of Nightwitch . . Well, some of them would fall for black magic, for a self-styled Satan who promised their wishes and desires would come true through the power of the Devil. Sabotage, that's something else again."

"Only requires one mon, John, to use a coven for his own ends."

"You mean someone, the Devil leader probably, encouraged the rebirth of the witch cult?"

"Enemy agents have been smuggled into our country along the Atlantic coast since even before the war started. Now if ye saw a stranger roaming the countryside hereabouts at an ungodly hour, ye mot be inclined to telephone the law or the FBI. But if ye saw a lad in a long black cloak, ye mot get back in bed and pull the covers over your head.

Figuring 'twas one of your warlock neighbors on his way to a meeting."

"Yes, I hadn't thought of that. I was digging into this chiefly because of the potential evil a gathering of witches can do," said the professor. "Even though black magic has no real power, a great deal of harm can be done in a community by those who believe it does."

"Aye, that's but one reason to put a stop to all this." Mac let out a pleased sigh. "There, I do believe it works on pressure from a mon's fingers, all ten. Stand back."

The wall made a slow grinding noise, shuffling open. There was a dimly lit stone hallway beyond.

"Think this is a way out?" whispered Ruyle.

"We'll try it, anyway," Mac told him.

The hooded figure walked, oblivious to the weather, to the slashing rain and wind, to the thunder and lightning.

All at once an extra portion of rain descended on the cloaked man.

A second later the Avenger dropped down out of the trees on him.

The man made no sound when Benson hit him. His sharp-featured face was blank, without expression, but he fought ferociously.

Snarling deep in his throat, the warlock clawed at the Avenger, snapped jagged teeth at his throat.

Benson twisted away, bent low. Using the man's arm as a lever, the Avenger threw him through the rain-filled night.

The cloaked figure, looking like an opening umbrella, sailed across the muddy road and slammed into the top rail of the rail fence.

Still making no sound, he dropped to the roadside and passed out.

The Avenger ran, vaulted the fence, and then dragged the unconscious man under it. He relieved him of his cloak and hood.

"Doggone," said Smitty, joining him, "the guy's more your size than mine."

Benson said nothing; he donned the cult robe.

"I think I ought to crash the party, too," said the giant.

"Wait here, back me up."

Smitty said, "Okay." He crouched beside the warlock and proceeded to tie him up.

The Avenger, shrouded in the cloak and hood, returned to the road. He went walking, stiff and straight, uphill into the darkness.

CHAPTER XX

Through The Wall

Nellie did not hesitate.

She crossed the room, stepped out into the hallway. "Cole?" she softly called.

He was nowhere to be seen. The long, shadowy hall was empty. Out here you could hear the steady beat of the rain more clearly.

Cole had a sense of humor, Nellie was well aware. But she didn't think he'd play a joke like this one on her. Not at a time when the lives of several people, including Mac, were at stake.

Which meant something had happened to him.

And if she weren't careful, it could well happen to her.

Carefully, she backed into the shrouded living room. Thunder exploded outside, farther away this time.

"Somebody had to sneak up on him," she told herself. "There's probably more than one secret opening in these old walls." She glanced around at the sheet-covered tables, chairs, and sofas.

She crossed to a shuttered window and tried to get a look at the darkness outside.

Then she heard it, almost lost in the noise made by the rain and the wind. A faint click.

Nellie did not turn around; she stayed at the window.

Five seconds passed.

She dropped to the floor on one knee, spun, and flashed the light upward.

The man who'd been approaching her with a blackjack ready to swing was taken by surprise. He jerked a hand up to shield his light-dazzled eyes.

Nellie reached out, caught hold of the blackjack hand. She pivoted, sent the stalker spinning across the dark room.

"Holy smokes!" He smacked into an empty bookcase, rotated, and tripped on the shroud over a fat chair. Muttering, he fell, entangled in the sheet, to the rug.

The deceptively sweet-seeming blonde was right after him. She grabbed him up, twisting one of his arms high behind his back. "Where is he?"

"Who?"

"My friend, the man who was with me."

"In the wall," answered the man, wincing. "Let up on that arm, that's my pitching arm, lady."

"That's right, I don't want to spoil your chances of playing on the prison team," said the girl. "How many of you are there?"

"Only me, lady. I'm the lookout here, case anybody comes snooping. Got me a nice little apartment fixed up underground. Only trouble is I have a heck of a time getting any of my favorite radio—"

"Where'd you leave my friend?"

"He's down in my place," answered the lookout. "I decked him while he was out in the hall. I got several different places I can step through the walls."

Planting a foot on the man's back, Nellie swiftly ripped up a sheet and tied him with it. Then she flashed the light around. The section of wall still hung half open.

"Lady," called the man as Nellie approached the entrance to the hidden passage, "don't leave me here, huh? This room gets awful damp. How about you drag me into the—"

Nellie stepped carefully into the wall.

There was a three-foot-wide passway there. It ran between the walls for about ten feet before dropping away into stairs. One hand shielding the light, the blonde moved along the passageway and went down the steps.

The stairway ended on a stone floor. Nellie calculated she was now roughly twenty feet underground. From up ahead somewhere she heard a moaning.

Silently, clicking off the light, she inched ahead.

Soneone was groaning and singing up there in the dark.

"Oh, my darling Nellie Gray, they have taken you away. And I'll never see my Nellie any more . . ."

"That's taken *her* away," Nellie corrected. She turned the flash back on, spotlighting the dazed Cole.

He was slumped against a wooden door, rubbing at the back of his head. "Ah, is that an angel of mercy come here to minister to me?"

"No, it's me, Nellie."

Shaking his head, yawning, Cole tried to stand. "Some chap gave me a clout on the sconce," he said.

"I know, he tried the same thing on me."

"But you manfully resisted, apparently." Wobbling, he got partway up.

"I had an advantage, I was expecting him." She put a hand out and felt his head. "A goose egg, but he didn't crack your skull. You'll be okay."

"I don't like to be trite and say what everybody says on these occasions," said Cole, "but where am I?"

"The mansion looks like it's a link with some kind of underground tunnel system," replied Nellie, taking another feel of his bump. "Yes, I'm sure you'll be okay."

"You overcame the lout who did this deed, you say?"

"Got him tied up in the living room."

"Would a bit of questioning be in order?"

"Maybe, but I think he's just another hireling," said the girl. "Somebody put here to see that only authorized personnel use the secret passages."

Taking the flash from her, Cole aimed the beam to his right. "Where would you guess these tunnels lead?"

"Well, since they left the kidnapped girl here, and since she doesn't seem to be around now, I'd say this is one way to get to witch headquarters."

Cole nodded, then grimaced. "Got to remember not to bob my head yet," he said. "Suppose, pixie, we follow this yellow brick road for a bit and see where it leads us."

"Maybe to where they're holding Mac," said Nellie.

Cole put his arm through hers. "Thanks, by the way, for the hairbreadth rescue," he said.

"It was nothing."

CHAPTER XXI

The Altar Of Sacrifice

The black-cloaked figure stooped to place a golden chalice beneath the trough in the stone altar. Tall black wax-encrusted candles, four of them, burned at the corners of the altar. In a gold censer grains of pungent incense burned, crackling and sputtering, sending up whirls of musky smoke. The walls of the huge abandoned barn had been hung with thick dark draperies. Rain pelted the peaked roof; thunder thumped.

Ten of the members of the coven were here, nine of them kneeling on the straw before the dark altar. The tenth, a gaunt woman of sixty, was making final adjustments to the trappings of the altar. When she finished, she joined the others, kneeling.

There was silence among the witches and warlocks. They knelt, eyes looking straight ahead, waiting. Three enormous rumbles of thunder shook the wooden walls of the old barn.

Then there was a new sound.

It cut across the silence, grating on the night air. A scream, a frightened, protesting scream.

Through the dark draperies at the rear of the altar came two dark-robed men. They carried Anne Barley between them. The girl's hands and feet were bound, but she managed to struggle. Hulda Dolittle, carrying a fat black candle, entered next. The rain, which had splashed at her robe, had extinguished the candle.

The witch walked to the altar and relit the candle from one of those that were burning there. As she held the flickering candle aloft, the two men carried Anne up and placed her atop the stone altar.

"Wake up, all of you!" cried the girl. "I don't know what they've given you, but you must snap out of this!"

Hulda placed her candle on a stand beside the altar, then went to kneel with the rest. The other two joined her.

Twisting so she could look down at them, Anne said, "You can't go ahead with this! Don't you understand?"

The coven, complete now, did not respond. They remained on their knees in the straw, watchful and, now, expectant.

"Sam, Sam Hollis!" called out Anne. "You're one of them, you're here. Sam, you have to stop this!"

Only silence answered her pleas.

Lightning crackled quite near to the barn; thunder boomed.

The Devil appeared.

Yellow smoke spewed up from behind the altar,

spiraling up to the eaves. Then the masked figure stood revealed, arms raised high in a triumphant gesture.

There was a low murmuring among the witches and warlocks.

In his right hand the masked Devil held a golden-handled knife.

The long, sharp blade of the sacrificial knife flared in the candlelight. The light played, too, on the mask and on the twisting horns.

In a booming voice which had something of the rumble of the thunder in it the Devil said, "No one can defy the Power."

"No one," repeated thirteen voices.

"All who defy the Power must perish."

"Perish."

"There is no stronger power on earth."

"None stronger."

"The Power of Satan."

"Satan."

"You see before you one who would destroy us."

"Destroy."

"She must pay."

"Pay."

"The price of blood!"

"Blood!"

"Stop it," cried Anne. "You chanting fools, you'll never get away with this."

"The hour is at hand," boomed the Devil.

"At hand," replied the congregation.

"The time is now!"

"Now!"

The knife began its fatal descent, driving down toward the girl's breast.

Then the knife was no longer in the Devil's hand.

It had gone spinning out of his fingers while the tip of the blade was still a foot from the girl.

The masked figure shouted with pain.

One of the robed men was standing. In his hand he held a strange pistol.

"Who dares defy me?" cried the Devil. "Who interferes with my plans?"

"I am known as the Avenger," said Benson in a resounding voice.

"Kill him!" ordered Satan.

A dozen cloaked figures converged on the Avenger. They struck him, clawed him, pulled him to the ground.

CHAPTER XXII

Labyrinth

"We're a-getting further beneath the earth," observed MacMurdie. "If this keeps on, we'll soon be shaking hands with the real Devil in person."

They were moving along a stone corridor that twisted downward. There was a light from a series of infrequent bulbs; air was fanned in through recently installed vents.

"I've been considering, Mac," said Dr. Ruyle, "this tunnel system. Most of the construction down here has to date back to the last century, at least, with the exception of the lights and the air-conditioning system, of course."

"Aye, John, that's so."

"I'd hazard a guess, therefore, that these passages were originally built for the use of smugglers who

112

thrived in this vicinity some hundred or so years ago."

"Then it's a good bet some of these tunnels lead to the water."

"Undoubtedly."

Mac nodded to himself. "There's probably been smuggling going on again, a new kind of smuggling."

"Foreign agents, you mean?"

"Aye, this witch nonsense is but a cover for a much worse business."

The two friends grew quiet, traveling on in silence until they reached the next intersection of tunnels.

"Which way now, Mac?"

The Scot scowled. " 'Tis a labyrinth we're in, for fair." He suddenly took hold of the professor's arm. "Back into that alcove, John."

Mac tugged his friend back the way they'd come.

From the right-hand forking of the tunnel came the faint sound of shuffling feet.

Then, soon, the murmur of voices drifted up to them.

"*Sicher und unversehrt,* Weidner," said one.

"*Ja,* we have been very lucky, Ulrich."

"It is as we were told," said Ulrich. "The scheme works."

"Let's hope you birds work out," said a third, gruffer, voice.

"Stay here until they pass," cautioned MacMurdie in a whisper.

If the men, three of them at least, continued on in the tunnel they were in, Mac would have a better chance to try what he had in mind. They might, though, come this way, meaning he and Ruyle would be spotted.

Eyes narrowed, holding his breath, Mac waited.

The men appeared at last, three of them, walking single file. The first two were garbed in dark cloaks and hoods, the third man wore a black raincoat and carried a shotgun.

The first man started to turn into MacMurdie's corridor.

"No, not that way," said the big man with the shotgun. "Keep on straight ahead."

"Sorry."

When the three had passed out of view, Mac made a wait-here gesture to Dr. Ruyle and left the shelter of the alcove.

Silently he moved in their wake. In seconds he narrowed the distance between himself and the rear man, the one with the double-barreled shotgun.

Mac closed in and made his move. He leaped for the big man, got one hand over his mouth and another on his throat. Deftly applied pressure knocked the man out. MacMurdie grabbed hold of the shotgun as the man tumbled to the ground.

"Was—?"

The two enemy agents had whirled around while their escort was dropping.

"Make not a move," warned Mac, turning the shotgun on them.

One of them had been reaching beneath his witch robe, "What are you—FBI?" he asked, raising his hands high.

"Just an interested private citizen, lad." Keeping the shotgun barrels leveled at them, the Scot called out, "John, I hae need of yer help."

The professor came running. "You caught them?"

"Aye, and now if ye'll help in getting them trussed up, we'll the sooner be on our way."

"I'm very disappointed, Ulrich."

"So am I," admitted his companion.

Mac and the professor, having left the three men tied and propped against a wall, were hurrying down the tunnel which should lead them to the harbor.

"I'm not even certain how long I've been down here," said Ruyle. "At any rate, it will be splendid to be above the ground once again."

MacMurdie, taking a sniff at the air, observed, "We're coming near to the ocean." He slowed his pace and brought the shotgun up into a more useful position.

"What do you intend to do when we're clear of this place?"

"We're nae clear yet," reminded the Scot. "We may have a bit more fighting to do."

"Seeing the way you handled those others, Mac, has made me an optimist."

MacMurdie motioned him to silence. He crouched, listening.

They could hear the outside now, the rain hitting the ground, wind scurrying through scrub brush. When they'd climbed a hundred yards farther, there ceased to be overhead lights.

The two men continued on for another hundred yards, around a bend, and then found their way blocked by a wooden door.

Mac pressed his ear against the wood. After a full minute he turned the handle and pulled the door open.

Beyond the door lay another stretch of tunnel, short and dark. The sound of the night rain was louder here, but no exit showed immediately.

Then something rattled, and a figure stepped through the thick brush that masked the tunnel mouth. "What's wrong, Hank?" The guard had a

115

flashlight in his hand. He turned it on, was raising it to shine on Mac and his friend.

The Scot jumped.

"What—"

Mac delivered two jabs to the guard's chin.

That caused him to drop the light. Three more jabs, and he himself fell.

"Now maybe we can take a look outside," said MacMurdie.

Before he could reach the masking brush, a submachine gun began to chatter immediately outside.

CHAPTER XXIII

A New Arrival

A few minutes prior to midnight someone had knocked on the front door of Chief Storm's white saltbox house. Roughly thirty seconds later, the phone down in the hall had commenced ringing.

"I knew it," said the police chief, rolling away from his slumbering wife. "I had a feeling something was going to break loose tonight."

With skating motions of his bare feet he located his slippers on the floor of the darkened bedroom. He snatched up his flannel bathrobe and seconds later was bounding down the stairway. "Hold on, everybody, hold on to your horses."

He had to pass the phone to reach the front door, so he took care of that first. "Chief Storm speaking."

"I'd like to talk to Agent Early."

"Who?"

"Agent Early, please."

"I . . . hold on a second." Leaving the receiver dangling, the chief trotted to the door.

A clean-cut young man in a tan raincoat was standing there. He held out an official identification card. "I'm Don Early."

"You got a telephone call." The chief pointed, with a thumb, at the wall phone.

"I hadn't expected it so soon." He gave the police chief a boyish smile before stepping into the hall. Taking up the receiver, he said, "Early."

"The tip was right. They landed, two men, approximately ten minutes ago."

"Okay, good. Don't close in on them. Wait till they lead us to their local contacts."

"Uh . . ."

"What?"

"We lost them."

Agent Early said, "You lost them?"

"Uh . . . they seemed to vanish."

"In a puff of smoke?"

"No, just vanished. We're going over the area, and I'll contact you again, soon as we come up with something."

"Do," said the federal agent. "I'll be down there myself soon." He hung up.

"Something's in the wind," observed Storm, coming down the hall to lean against the newel post.

"Came here to ask your cooperation."

"What's up? Sounds like something pretty important."

"Espionage," Early told him. "Two enemy agents were landed from a U-boat in the harbor tonight."

"Yep, that is pretty important."

"Not the first time."

The chief blinked. "I should of known about this."

118

"So should we," said the clean-cut agent. "If we hadn't received a tip we wouldn't have known about this landing tonight, either."

"Who told you 'bout it?"

"Don't know, yet."

Rubbing his eyes, Chief Storm asked, "What can I do to help out, Mr. Early?"

"How many men do you have on your force?"

"Only me and an assistant," answered Chief Storm. "Of course I could ring up the Civil Defense fellers, we got six air raid wardens."

Early scratched at his rain-dampened crewcut. "Not yet," he said. "Wanted you to know I was in the area, mainly." He took a few steps toward the doorway. "You know the beach area fairly well?"

"Ought to, after living here nearly forty years."

"The two spies who came ashore, my men lost track of them," said Early. "Any idea where they might hide?"

For several seconds the chief's face was blank, then he remembered something. "The pirate caves," he said.

"Pirate caves?"

"Well, sir, now, they weren't actual pirate caves, but I remember we called them that when I was a young feller playing down there," explained Chief Storm. "They was the mouths of some kind of tunnels. We always meant to explore them all, through and through, but we never did. I think maybe we was a mite scared. Darn, I ain't thought of those for years. Don't think the young kids nowadays even know about the pirate caves, since nobody uses that stretch of beach for swimming no more."

"Sounds like a good possibility," said Agent Early. "Can you take me there, Chief, show me where the tunnels are?"

119

"Might take me a while, till the kid I was way back then helps me remember," said Storm. "But, yep, I'm sure I can. You just wait till I pull on some clothes." He started up the stairs, then stopped. "Say now . . .?"

"Yes?"

"Thought just now struck me," said the chief. "I wonder if these disappearance cases I been working on are tied in with your espionage thing."

"Somebody's disappeared?"

Chief Storm nodded glumly. "Three folks, so far," he said. "And then there's two dead men and the other four Mr. Benson turned over to me. Course he didn't say nothing about them being spies. But still, now that my brain's all woke up, it does seem—"

"Benson?" asked Early, a look of fretful anticipation touching his youthful face. "That wouldn't be Richard Henry Benson?"

"Yep, that's him, very soft-spoken feller," replied the chief.

"Why is Benson in Nightwitch?"

"Something to with his friend Mr. MacMurdie vanishing and—"

"MacMurdie's here, too?"

"Well, we ain't sure. He was here, but then he wasn't. Or so it seemed," said Chief Storm. "Mr. Benson promised to give me all the details tomorrow."

"Then he's planning something tonight," said Early. "Damn, how'd he get onto this ahead of us?"

"You think he's after them saboteurs, too?"

"Why else would the Avenger be here?" said the federal agent.

CHAPTER XXIV

Reunion

"Perhaps it's only this spooky atmosphere," said Cole, "but I think I heard a girl scream."

"So did I," replied Nellie.

The pair had been traveling along dim passways of rock for several minutes now.

"Up ahead that way," said Cole, "unless my old ears deceive me."

"It could be the missing girl. Let's go." Nellie broke into a run.

Cole caught up with her after a moment of concerted sprinting. "We ought to enter you in a marathon, Nell."

"I'd get bored with twenty-six miles of just running."

The tunnel they came into now slanted sharply upward. It was empty, but the scream sounded again. They stopped for a moment.

"This," said Cole in a low voice, "must be an egress that leads to the world outside."

"Listen to that," said the little blonde. "Someone shouting, others chanting."

"I don't think this is the weekly meeting of the Browning Society we find ourselves underneath, princess. It's tonight's Black Mass." He broke into a jog again.

"We've got to stop that sacrifice," said Nellie, catching up with him.

"Tread softly now," he cautioned as they reached the dead end of the tunnel. "We don't want to spoil Richard's play. If all went well, he's up there mingling with the Lucifer fans right now."

"Well, at least let's get into a position to lend a hand, if need be."

Cole was stretching up, exploring the ceiling with the flashlight. "Ah, here's a trapdoor," he announced.

The chanting above them grew louder, more frenzied.

"Must be a way into their meeting hall," said Nellie.

"Climb upon my hand, pixie, and I'll boost you up."

"Let's hope I don't emerge smack dab in the middle of the sacrificial altar." She placed a foot in Cole's interlocked hands.

"Going up."

"Ouch." Nellie's blonde head had tapped into the wood boards of the trapdoor. "Okay, there's a bolt to throw. There. Now, I'll ease this darn thing open. Stand by to duck."

She had raised the door a cautious inch when a single shot rang out in the barn above.

Then a voice commanded, "Kill him!"

Smitty, as the time since the Avenger's departure lengthened, grew more and more impatient. Normally the giant could sit calmly for hours working on some mechanical problem in the lab. But when he sensed a brawl might be in the offing, he was restless until he was where it was going to be.

And it wasn't going to be out here, he didn't think. Not hunkered down here among the trees with the collar of his overcoat getting soggy and the rain spilling down off his hat brim.

Dick Benson had been gone over ten minutes. Smitty was getting that itchy feeling. Something was going to happen, and he wanted to be there.

He left the shelter of the woods and trotted in the direction the Avenger had gone. A few moments later, as lightning obligingly lit up the countryside, Smitty saw the old barn where the witches were meeting.

"Not so much as a dab of light showing," he said to himself. "They must have their blackout curtains up good."

He worked his way across the rain-washed field, stopping behind a collapsed cultivator rig which looked now like the huge skeleton of some long-extinct beast.

After watching the barn for a minute, the giant ran to it. He was crouched outside, his face near the wide door, when he heard a single shot from inside.

And a voice ordering, "Kill him!"

"You ought to wear a hat," suggested Chief Storm as he and the federal agent slogged along the muddy midnight beach. He tapped the stiff oilskin hat on his own head. "That's what causes colds and the grippe, not wearing hats."

"Never liked hats."

123

They'd already passed two of the men Early had watching the harbor. He'd signaled them to follow him, at a distance.

"All coming back to me," said the chief. He gestured, pointing through the rain. "Ought to be right up here."

"What would these tunnels have been built for in the first place?"

The chief shrugged, and rain spattered off his glazed headgear. "Most likely it was the smugglers who used this port back in the 1800s. See, the nineteenth century was a more leisurely time, and so folks had time to build all kinds of things." He halted, frowning around. "This ain't quite right." After glancing back at the foamy sea, he began walking up the scrubby hillside. "Yep, this is the way. And that should be one of—"

"Down!" Early tripped the chief and threw himself to the ground beside him.

Machine-gun fire raked the place where they had been standing.

"Looks like we're at the right place," said the police chief, spitting out mud.

"I'm a federal agent," called Early through cupped hands. "Put down that gun."

The machine gun barked again, sending spurts of mud flying up in a line a few feet in front of them.

Early got his .38 revolver out of his shoulder holster. "I'm giving you one more chance," he shouted.

The figure with the machine gun, who was crouching at the mouth of a tunnel, suddenly made a whooping sound. He stood up, looked as though he were attempting to fly up into the rainy night by flapping his arms. The submachine gun fell into a clump of bushes.

124

"Who be ye down there?" asked a voice up there in the darkness.'

"Don Early," called the FBI man. "I'm a federal agent."

"Aye, I've heered of you, lad," said MacMurdie. "We've near crossed paths afore."

"MacMurdie?" said the agent, tentatively standing up.

" 'Tis indeed." Mac let go of the guard he'd just now rendered unconscious. He came downhill toward the two men. "And I've my friend John Ruyle wi' me."

"Well, sir," remarked Chief Storm as he helped himself up off the dirt, "that's two of my missing persons I can stop looking for."

"Would ye be interested in a couple Nazi spies, Mr. Early?" asked Mac when he neared them.

"You know where they are?"

"They should be back in yon tunnel, all wrapped up and a-waiting for ye."

"It's good to see you again, Chief Storm," said Dr. Ruyle, joining the group.

"I'm right sorry I didn't find you myself, John. Makes me feel sort of sheepish, it does."

Agent Early beckoned the rest of his men—there were five of them all together—to close in around him. "What's underground there, MacMurdie?"

"Spies, fer one thing, lad," replied the Scot. "And, I do believe, if we find the right tunnel we'll also find us a coven of witches."

"Witches?" said Early.

The Avenger brought up his knees, connecting with the chin of the man who was leaping for him. He rolled across the straw flooring, doffing the

125

cloak. Leaping to his feet, he flung it at the three who were closest to him.

The dark, billowing cloth engulfed two of the men, but the third man stepped clear. There was a vicious-looking knife in his hand.

"Kill him!" roared the Devil. "That man must die!"

The Avenger fired his unique little pistol again. The slug grazed the approaching knifer's hand, causing him to drop the weapon and howl.

But more of them, women now as well as men, were making for him. Frenzied they were, eyes burning bright.

"Naw, this ain't no fair," Smitty pointed out. The giant had smashed his way into the barn. He began grabbing the robed figures and tossing them aside.

Smitty tossed men and women alike, though when he recognized one of his opponents as a woman he always added, " 'Scuse me, ma'am."

"These two must never leave here alive!" warned the Devil. "You must kill them. It is my command!"

From a fold in his robe Satan drew a pistol of his own, a silver-handled .32. Bracing his elbows on the stone altar, he took careful aim at the fighting figure of Dick Benson.

The Devil waited patiently until he would have a clear shot at the Avenger, could see him free of the swirling, entangling robes of his disciples.

"That's not at all sporting, old fellow." Cole Wilson appeared next to the Devil and chopped at his elbow.

The masked man dropped the pistol onto the stone and whirled to face Cole. "Fool, you dare defy me?"

"Ever since I saw *King Kong* seven times in my

126

youth, I've been immune to shaggy monsters, old boy."

With a swift darting movement of one hand, Satan threw the golden container of smoldering incense into Cole's face.

Cole fell back, slapping at the smoky mass, wiping it from his face and eyes.

The Devil grabbed up the girl, Anne Barley, and ran.

Nellie, who'd let Cole come up into the big barn ahead of her, popped through the floor now.

The Devil wasn't going to use that exit, though. He was making for another corner of the barn.

Sending up flecks of straw, Nellie speeded after him.

Before she reached the fleeing figure and the girl, a hooded witch—one of those Smitty had tossed aside—got up and made a wobbling tackle.

It wasn't a good tackle, but it was sufficient to knock the little blonde down. That gave the Devil time to escape through another trapdoor.

Five seconds after he dropped into the ground, there was a huge explosion from below. The entire trapdoor came flying up into the candle-lit barn. Smoke spewed up, billowing.

"Looks as though we won't be able to follow His Satanic Majesty that way," said Cole. "He must have had a charge of explosives ready to close this end in case he was ever pursued."

"Idiot, your hair's still on fire," said Nellie, reaching up and slapping at his head.

"So that's what that smell was. With all this incense and candle smoke, not to mention the more familiar barn smells, I wasn't sure what it was."

"There, it's out," said the blonde. She brushed at

127

his cheek. "Your good looks are relatively unim-
paired."

"My reputation isn't in very good shape," he said.
"We shouldn't have let him take off with the young
lady."

"Hiya, Nellie," said Smitty. He came over to
them, rubbing his huge palms together. "I think
that's it. How many witches in a coven?"

"I think you've got them all," said Cole, surveying
the giant's handiwork. All of the robed figures were
stretched out on the floor, each one neatly tied.

The Avenger was pulling back the hood from
each face. "Satan himself got away," he said.

"My fault, Richard," said Cole. "I should have
been expecting more dirty tricks."

"We have a fairly clear idea who's been posing as
the Devil here," said Benson. "I'm certain we'll
bring him to justice very soon."

"He might hurt that girl," said Smitty.

"No, he probably intends to use her as a hostage," said the Avenger. "She's no use to him dead.
So we still have time. And now—"

"Woosh, 'tis a pity," came the voice of MacMurdie. "All the folderol is over."

"Mac," cried Nellie, running over to him, "you're
alive!"

"Aye," said the Scot, who had just climbed up
through the same trapdoor Nellie and Cole had
used, "and 'tis not ever' man who's spent a day in a
tomb who can make that claim, lass."

The little blonde hugged him and kissed him on
the cheek.

"You should disappear more often, Fergus,"
grinned Cole.

" 'Tis no way to spend a vacation." Mac turned,
bent, and held out his hand to John Ruyle.

128

The professor climbed up, then assisted Don Early.

"Don't understand it," said the federal agent. "You keep beating me to the punch, Benson."

The Avenger crossed the barn to shake hands with Early. "Only by a few minutes, it seems," he said. "These people here are all members of the Nightwitch cult. I think you'll find most of them have nothing to do with the smuggling of espionage agents into the country. Only Satan and one or two others were aware of what all this was really about."

Early ran his fingers along the top of the stone altar. "Mean there's been an honest-to-gosh witch cult flourishing around here?"

"For quite some time," said Benson.

"The old beliefs die hard," said Dr. Ruyle.

"Especially when they can be put to modern uses," said the Avenger.

CHAPTER XXV

The Devil's Domain

Rain worked down through the cracks in the gray stone roof of the tunnel. The rapidly dripping water made muddy puddles on the floor.

The masked Devil dropped the struggling Anne Barley onto the floor. Muddy water splashed.

"Don't you realize it's all over?" the girl said. "That was the Avenger up there. You'll never—"

"Please be quiet, Anne." Satan took hold of a metal wheel set in the wall and twisted it.

The stone wall swung open. The Devil dragged the girl through the narrow opening.

They emerged into a large damp room, its tall windows boarded. There were rows of ruined pews and a dusty pulpit.

"This is the old Olmstead Hill Church," realized the girl.

"The last place anyone would think of looking for

the Devil." He dragged her to the center aisle and left her there, still securely tied. "I doubt they'll think to look for you here, either."

"You can't gain anything by this. They'll catch you. If you're thinking of using me as a hostage, you—"

"I have absolutely no need of a hostage." He took hold of the hideous mask and yanked it free of his head. "You're merely part of a subterfuge."

"Sam Hollis," said Anne, "I didn't think, even after I knew you were one of them, that you were—"

"The leader?" The editor chuckled. "No, that's because of the part I've been playing here. A good man, Sam Hollis, but not really quite first-caliber. Plenty good for a small town like Nightwitch, but probably couldn't make it in Boston or Hartford." He took off his robe.

"You said you weren't going to use me as a hostage? Do you mean—"

"I'm not even going to kill you now, Anne," said the gaunt-faced Hollis. "It serves no purpose. The simple locals who were persuaded to join the cult, to participate in the forbidden rites and ask the Devil for small favors, those fools who willingly took the drugs that made them even more docile and obedient, they would have been impressed by a blood sacrifice. The Avenger spoiled the show, so I will merely leave you here." His chuckle turned into a laugh. "I'm sure they'll think I'm holding you hostage, waiting for them to close in so I can use you to bargain with. That's the furthest thing from my mind."

"You don't expect to walk away," she said. "They know who you—"

"Ah, no, that's where you're wrong. No one, at

least no one at the Nightwitch level of the operation, knows what face was behind the mask," said Hollis. "I'll be able to return to my office and continue being well-meaning Sam. In a few days, when things have quieted down, I'll move on. Accept a better offer from a newspaper someplace else. That will be that."

Anne said, as he moved toward the still open door in the wall, "Nobody ever comes to this old church, there's nothing nearby."

"Yes, exactly, Anne."

She shook her head. "Even so, you won't get away."

"You'll never know," he told her—and stepped through the wall.

Cole Wilson rubbed his foot over the wood floor beside the potbellied stove. Something grated underfoot. "It is rather vexing, isn't it?" he said to Sam Hollis.

The editor was behind his desk. The day was clear, moving toward noon. "Can't figure it," he said, watching the two men from Justice, Inc. "This self-styled Satan has had Anne for nearly twelve hours, you say, and still hasn't made any move. Doesn't make sense."

Smitty said, "Could be he's waiting till we close in on him. He sure hasn't made any demands. And all the routes out of here are being watched, you can bet."

"Poor Anne. I hope—excuse me." The phone on his desk had rung.

When he turned to pick it up, Cole bent and scooped up the gritty substance he'd noticed on the floor. Cole, grinning, tipped a nod at the giant.

"Yes, they are," said Hollis into the phone. "Cer-

132

tainly. A call for you, Smitty," He handed the phone across to the big man.

"Yeah? They did, huh? Hey, that's great. Then it's only a matter of closing in, huh? Great." When Smitty handed the phone back to the editor he slipped. He fell hard, chin slamming into desk top. He let go the phone and clutched at the editor to keep from falling to the floor.

"Less than graceful, Smitty," said Cole, dropping the grains of incense into his jacket pocket.

"Gee, I'm awful sorry, Mr. Hollis." The big man had regained his balance and was smoothing out the papers he'd scattered.

"No damage done," assured Hollis. "That call must have got you pretty excited."

Smitty studied his shoes. "Gosh, you put me in a funny position, Mr. Hollis," he said finally. "I mean, you been very helpful to us and I know you're as worried about Anne Barley as anybody. But I don't know—"

"Is it an important break?" asked Cole.

"Well, yeah," admitted the giant. "Thing is, I don't think it ought to get into the papers until we're sure."

Hollis chuckled. "I'm not interested in scoops in this case, Smitty. If there's something about Anne you feel you can tell me, I'd surely like to hear it. You can bet it won't go any further, and it won't be in the *Guardian* without everyone's okay."

"I think we can confide in Mr. Hollis, " said Cole. "Besides, you've got my curiosity aroused."

"That was Dick Benson on the phone," said Smitty. "He says that Don Early guy, the big hush-hush government guy, just got another tip. From the same person who tipped him off about that spy landing last night. Seems like Early knows where

133

Anne Barley is being held. He's heading for there right now."

"Without us?" asked Cole.

"You know how Early is, always wants to be one jump ahead of Justice, Inc."

Hollis stood up. "Well, that is good news. I'm going to keep my fingers crossed for Anne," he said. "If you'll excuse me, I have an early lunch date with one of our local boosters."

When the team was out on the street, Cole asked, "Did you plant the bug?"

"Sure I did. You didn't think I was doing all that clumsy stuff just to amuse you, did you?"

"Let's pop into our automobile and get ready to tail Mr. Hollis and his newly acquired tracking device," said Cole, heading for the corner.

"Right with you," said Smitty. "What was that stuff you sneaked off his floor?"

"You really are a heathen, Smitty. That was incense, my boy," said Cole. "When Mr. Lucifer Satan flung a bowl of it in my face last evening, some of it must have clung to him, gotten in his shoes or his pants cuffs. One more item that leads me to believe he is the Devil we seek."

Smitty grabbed open the car door and jumped in behind the wheel.

The long black car turned away from the sea and began climbing uphill. Nellie drove, while the Avenger sat in the back seat with a survey map of the town spread out on his lap.

In his hand he held the miniature two-way belt radio. "Yes, I've got you located, Cole."

"Drat," came Cole's voice out of the speaker, "what's the name of this street we just turned onto?"

"Mott's Hill Road," supplied Smitty.

134

"Mr. Hollis and his bug are leading us up Mott's Hill Road," said Cole. "This little tracking box of Smitty's is performing admirably."

Benson leaned forward to tell Nellie, "Turn left at the next corner."

She obliged.

"And so," continued Cole, "we once again are leaving the comforts of civilization behind as we penetrate into the vast unexplored wilderness. We've left the settled part of town, Richard, and we're going North on High Valley Road."

The Avenger located the spot on the map before him. "We'll intersect that if we stay on the road we're on now, Nellie."

The girl nodded, saying, "What do you think Hollis was planning to do with the girl?"

"Perhaps nothing," said Benson. "He may simply have left her where he's heading now, to use as a trump card if necessary."

"He's got guts," said Nellie, "brazening it out and walking right back to his old job. Just as though nothing had happened."

"As far as he knows, no one is aware he's the Devil in this setup," said Benson. "You sat in on some of the questioning of the witches and warlocks last night. Not one of them had any idea of who was the leader of the cult."

"Anne Barley must know, by now."

"Probably, which is why Hollis is going to try to beat the government to her," said Benson. "If she dies before anyone can talk to her, he's in the clear."

"Our fox has stopped his run," announced Cole from the miniature radio.

"Where?"

"Doesn't appear to be anything hereabouts at all, Richard," replied Cole. "Can't actually see his car as yet . . . ah, there he is, parking on a dirt road in the middle of nowhere. We're on Olmstead Hill Road now. Smitty and I are driving on by, trying very hard to look like a pair of maiden ladies interested solely in gravestone rubbings. We'll park out of his sight and double back on foot to—Aha, he just sprang from his vehicle clutching what appears to be a high-powered rifle! Find us a parking space, Smitty."

"Keep in contact, Cole," said the Avenger.

"Looks like our bluff is going to work," said Nellie. "If we're in time to save Anne Barley."

"I think we will be," he said. "It was obvious that the leader of this whole venture, the man who played the Devil, had to be either Sam Hollis or Gil Lunden. They were the only ones who could have set up all the traps. So we tried the same bluff on both of them. Smitty and Cole called on Hollis, Mac looked in on Lunden. Lunden didn't take the bait."

"I'm glad, since he's obviously the love interest in all this," said Nellie. "I favor adventures that end with a clinch."

"Richard, we're hoofing it and we can see Hollis moving, very very cautiously, through a bit of woodland up ahead," reported Cole.

The Avenger consulted his map. "There's an abandoned church, according to this map, below that particular patch of woods, Cole," he said into the radio. "That may be where he's heading."

"Unless he's merely out for a tramp in the woods," said Cole. "Yes, he looks to be sneaking up with his rifle to make sure he takes care of any G-men in the vicinity."

"We should be there in five minutes," said the Avenger. "Keep on his trail."

"I intend to," said Cole. "I want to get a better look at this Barley girl, anyway."

Anne looked up expectantly. Someone was pounding on the church doors. "Help, I'm in here!" she cried out.

The boards that held the doors shut gave way. "Save your breath, Anne," said Hollis. "It isn't a rescue at all." He stepped, roughly, over the smashed boards.

"What do you want?"

The rawboned man was perspiring freely. He wiped a sleeve across his forehead. Some of his confidence seemed to have left him. He glanced around anxiously. "They don't appear to be here yet," he said finally. "Which gives me some time, how much I don't know."

"I don't—"

Hollis stomped down the church aisle. "Somehow, don't ask me how, they know you're here," he said, panting. "But that doesn't matter, because if they find you dead, it makes no difference. Dead, you can't possibly tell them."

"Sam, you can't—"

"Stop telling me what I can and can't do," he told her. "I've got to kill you, Anne. Right now, before you tell anyone." He turned the rifle on her.

"Sam, for the love of—"

"Ow!" Hollis's arms went flying up, causing him to hold the rifle for an instant as though it were a chinning bar. His breath coughed out of him, and he stumbled against a pew.

The cause of all this was Cole Wilson, who had come plummeting down from the organ loft up above. "I thought we cured you of the sacrifice habit last evening, old man." He grabbed the rifle away from Hollis and threw it aside.

Hollis fell to one knee, caught hold of the side of

137

a pew, and pulled himself to his feet. "You conned me," he accused.

"Oh, yes, to be sure," Cole moved a hand toward the pistol beneath his coat.

Hollis lowered his head and butted into Cole. "I'm still going to get clear."

It took Cole a few seconds to catch his breath. Then he took off after Hollis. The gaunt editor was running for the rear of the church.

Cole narrowed the distance between them. He sprang, tackled Hollis and brought him down.

Hollis thrashed around on the floor, kicking at Cole. One foot managed to connect with Cole's chin.

The young man let go and brought his hands up toward his face. Hollis scrambled to his feet. He almost made it to the way out.

Smitty was there, arms folded. "We got you, Hollis," he said.

The fleeing editor made a final try. He went for a hand gun inside his jacket.

"No, you don't!" Smitty stepped into the aisle from outside, swinging.

One punch, which connected with Hollis's jaw, felled him.

"That takes care of the Devil," said Smitty.

"Another fall from grace." Cole was up and around, making his way to the bound girl. "Permit me to introduce myself, Miss Barley. I'm Cole Wilson." He located his pocketknife and went to work on the ropes that held her.

"Thank you," she said in a faint voice. "I thought for certain it was all over."

"We couldn't let the powers of darkness triumph," Cole said. "I do apologize, however, for my rather bravura entrance. I didn't want to come in the same way Hollis had, and then I happened to

138

notice a window up there that wasn't boarded. Smitty boosted me up to it."

"I'm Smitty," said the giant. While Cole was releasing the girl, he had trussed up Hollis.

"I've heard of you, both of you," said Anne. "You're colleagues of Mr. MacMurdie's, members of Justice, Inc."

"The same," admitted Cole. "There, that's the last of the ropes. Let me rub your limbs, Miss Barley, to restore circulation."

"Thank you. About last night . . ." she said. "I'm somewhat hazy about what actually happened. Is everyone all right?"

"Sure," Smitty told her, leaning a big elbow against the nearby pulpit. "Mac's safe, and so is his buddy Doc Ruyle. We rounded up all the witches, and all the spies. Well, at least the most recent batch. Now that we got the kingpin himself, we should be able to track down the rest of the Nazi agents he's been helping ashore here in Nightwitch."

"I might add," added Cole, "that young Gil Lunden is also in tip-top shape and most anxious about your safety."

"Oh, him," said Anne.

A grin appeared on Cole's face and grew wider. "Here's my arm, Miss Barley," he offered. "I'll escort you to the outside."

Arm in arm the two of them walked down the aisle.

CHAPTER XXVI

Departures

MacMurdie wiped his mouth with the checkered napkin. "That was a breakfast of almost prewar quality," he said, leaning back. "Except for their spurious coffee."

It was a new morning, the day after they had located Anne Barley in the old church and captured the Nightwitch Devil.

Mac, Nellie, Smitty, and Richard Benson were seated around a table in a small inn near the shore.

"What are you figuring to do now, Mac?" the giant wanted to know.

"I thought I mot stay on here for a few days," replied the Scot. " 'Tis still m' vacation, ye know."

"You spent the first part of it in some interesting places," said Nellie, looking again toward the door.

"Aye, not ever' tourist gets to spend a night in a tomb, or in a smuggler's tunnel system."

Smitty took a sip of his coffee. "I'm kind of worried about my own trip," he said.

"Aye, I forgot ye're going out to California next month."

"Yeah, to see a couple old buddies of mine who'll be on leave from the Air Corps," said the big man. He tugged at his ear. 'I don't know, though, Mac. Seems like every time one of us takes a trip, something goes blooey. Like Nellie went up to Connecticut last year and we got tangled up in that werewolf business, and then when Cole was out in California—"

"Ye've nothing to worry about, lad," MacMurdie assured him. "Those were mere coincidences."

"And you've got to admit," said Benson, "that you enjoy a good brawl, Smitty."

"Sure, I suppose so, Dick," said Smitty. "Still, it might be nice to spend a whole week without running into anything odd and goofy."

"Dull," said Nellie. "I know before I joined the crew, life was sort of monotonous."

Mac turned to the Avenger, "Ye'll not be needing me, Richard?"

"Not for a few days, Mac. I'll be involved in helping round up the remaining members of the spy ring," said Benson. "The ones scattered around New England."

"Ye got a hefty list of names from that skurlie Hollis," said MacMurdie.

The Avenger nodded.

Nellie was watching the door again. "Here comes Cole."

The grinning young man sauntered over and took the one empty chair. "How's the coffee, Mac?"

"Most foul."

"Well?" said Nellie.

141

"Miss Barley sends you all her best wishes," said Cole. "She and I had a very charming breakfast at the Old Fiddler's Inn."

"It's incredible," said the little blonde. "I didn't think, for a while there, you were even going to meet her, and here you are romancing her."

"Ah, pixie, hotcakes and maple syrup, or an imitation thereof, is not romance," said Cole. "I merely sensed that the girl needed someone to confide in, a shoulder to cry on, as they phrase it in the Bette Davis films. So I provided."

Smitty asked, "What's she got to cry about now?"

"Life in Nightwitch," said Cole. "Now that there's no more witches to track, Anne feels life here is going to be dull and monotonous."

"She's got her dashing attorney," Nellie pointed out.

"In her opinion, which seems quite sound, Gil Lunden can not accurately be described as dashing, Nell," Cole said. "No, for real dash, one has to look further afield. Possibly to some teeming metropolis."

"You didn't talk her into leaving Nightwitch for Manhattan?"

"Not at all, princess. She's going to try Boston first." Cole lifted the coffee pot off the warmer and filled the empty cup at his place. "Of course, Boston, even in these days of restricted travel, is not that far from New York City."

"What's she going to do in Boston?"

"Work on one of the newspapers. They're quite keen to have her do a several-part series about the witches of Nightwitch, the parts of the story that can safely be told, that is." He sampled the coffee. "Not exactly foul, Mac, but bordering on it."

Nellie put her elbows on the table top and rested her chin on her hands. "I was hoping for a romantic finish to this case. Now you tell me they're breaking up."

"Apparently the chap's reaction to her sleuthing tipped the scales in favor of departure," said Cole. "Besides which, with Hollis in the pokey, she's got no boss at the moment."

"You want to drive back to the city with me?" Smitty asked him. "Or are you planning more romantic interludes?"

"I am, as the popular dirge from New Orleans has it, free as a bird, Smitty. I stand ready to depart at any time."

"Oops," said Nellie. "Here comes that spit-and-polish boy from Washington, D.C."

Don Early, tan raincoat over his arm, was approaching their table. "Good morning," he said, favoring them all with one of his youthful smiles.

"Care to join us?" asked Benson.

"Only dropped by to say so long," said Early. "I've got to get back to Washington on a new job and . . ." He paused, looked at the Avenger. "Where are you going next?"

"Back to Manhattan, eventually," answered Benson.

Letting out a sigh, Early said, "Won't run into you on this next one, then. And that'll give me a chance to solve it myself." He smiled once more. "Not that I don't appreciate your help, not that the government doesn't. Like to come in first sometimes, though. Understand?"

"Perfectly," answered the Avenger.

"But you're going to be in New England and then New York," said the government agent. "So I can't possibly run into you in California this time. Right?"

"I'm going to—" began Smitty. A nudge from Nellie halted him.

"Good," said Early, not catching what the giant had started to say. "Thanks again. Bye." He walked, with a confident lilt in his step, out of the inn.

"California," said Smitty, scowling. "What'd I tell you?"

Silhouette®

Romantic
SUSPENSE

*Excitement, danger
and passion guaranteed!*

USA TODAY bestselling author
Marie Ferrarella
is back with the second installment
in her popular miniseries,
*The Doctors Pulaski: Medicine
just got more interesting...*
DIAGNOSIS: DANGER is on sale
April 2007 from Silhouette®
Romantic Suspense (formerly
Silhouette Intimate Moments).

*Look for it wherever
you buy books!*

COMING NEXT MONTH FROM

HARLEQUIN®
HISTORICAL

- **THE WICKED EARL**
by **Margaret McPhee**
(Regency)
When a handsome stranger saves her from the clutches of a rake,
Madeline is too relieved to suspect that her tall, dark defender may
have a less-than-reputable reputation....

- **BRIDE OF SHADOW CANYON**
by **Stacey Kayne**
(Western)
Whatever he believed about the saloon singer's shady past, Jed
would protect her future with his life!

- **COMMANDED TO HIS BED**
by **Denise Lynn**
(Medieval)
Wedded, but never bedded, the lady Adrienna cannot trust the
husband she hardly knows. But how can she resist his seductive
passion?

- **THE VAGABOND DUCHESS**
by **Claire Thornton**
(Restoration)
Practical Temperance only wanted to find her baby's father. She
didn't know that the irresistible rogue who'd comforted her as
London burned was a *duke!*
*City of Flames—Smoldering desire at the heart of a burning
London!*

HHCNM0307